James Benjamin Blish wa
studied zoology at Rutge
years in the US Army. D
he moved with his family

His prolific output in
original *Star Trek* TV scripts and many
novels, amongst them *A Case of Conscience*, for which he
won a Hugo Award in 1959.

Also by James Blish

Novels

And All the Stars a Stage
Black Easter (Faust Aleph-Null)
A Case of Conscience
Cities in Flight
The Triumph of Time (A Clash of Cymbals)
Doctor Mirabilis
The Duplicated Man
Earthman Come Home
Jack of Eagles
Midsummer Century
Mission to the Heart Stars
The Night Shapes
The Quincunx of Time
The Seedling Stars
The Star Dwellers
Year 2018! (They Shall Have Stars)
Titan's Daughter
A Torrent of Faces
The Vanished Jet
Vor
The Warriors of Day

Short Story Collections

Anywhen
Best Science Fiction Stories of James Blish
Galactic Cluster
So Close to Home

James Blish

Get Out of My Sky

and

There Shall Be No Darkness

PANTHER
GRANADA PUBLISHING
London Toronto Sydney New York

Published by Granada Publishing Limited
in Panther Books 1980

ISBN 0 586 04817 0

A Panther UK Original
Get Out of My Sky first published in the USA by
Street & Smith Pubs. Inc. 1957

There Shall Be No Darkness first published in
Great Britain by Faber & Faber 1965

Granada Publishing Limited
Frogmore, St Albans, Herts AL2 2NF
and
3 Upper James Street, London W1R 4BP
866 United Nations Plaza, New York, NY 10017, USA
117 York Street, Sydney, NSW 2000, Australia
100 Skyway Avenue, Rexdale, Ontario, M9W 3A6, Canada
PO Box 84165, Greenside, 2034 Johannesburg, South Africa
CML Centre, Queen & Wyndham, Auckland 1, New Zealand

Set, printed and bound in Great Britain by
Cox & Wyman Ltd, Reading
Set in Intertype Times

Contents

Get Out of My Sky

It was like a kind of dance, with the sighs and shouts and drumming feet of the crowd for music. The little figure on the platform, far away at the centre of the huge pavilion, moved from one edge of the boards to another with desperation, his legs moving loosely, his arms flapping, the white blur of his face turned appealingly to the tented sky and then to the swaying audience.

The young couple at the back could hear his voice, but not what he was saying. Only the wavering sound of someone shouting penetrated this far through the sea-roar of the crowd. They looked at each other apprehensively. They had debated whether or not to come to this meeting, and others like it, for a long time. They loved the man on the platform, and they had not, at first, wanted to see him doing what he was doing now – dancing and pleading before a packed mass of overwrought humanity, saying things that nobody but those in the front row could hear with any accuracy, yet which somehow moved the entire mass.

In the end a morbid curiosity had won, and here they were, listening – but to what? Just a moment ago, the man had fallen on his knees at one border of the stage and held out his arms; a great groan of orgiastic sorrow was spreading from the people closest to that side of the platform, beating its way outwards through the pavilion in a wave of contagion. It was still coming like a foaming comber towards the young couple when the man on the platform was on his feet again, striding towards the great central pole which held the tent's pyramidal vault in place. He shook his fist at it, and then at the sky. After a moment's hesitation – which compelled instant silence in the centre of the audience, a silence which was itself audible out here at the roaring periphery (like, the young man thought incongruously, the hole in a doughnut) – he rushed on to seize the ridgepole itself, in what was apparently an insane effort to wrestle the immense duralumin mast bodily out of the ground.

The whole crowd was on its feet in an instant, screaming. Fists were being shaken aloft everywhere. A chanting began near the centre of the tent and was rocking the entire enclosure within five seconds.

Get out of our sky! Get out of our sky! Get out of our sky!

The young couple were standing and shouting with the rest, though the words filled them with terror. The whole world of Home tipped and reeled to the rhythm of that massive chant. There was no questioning it. It was the reason why the universe existed. It was the purest of transports, a vast exultation of hatred.

Get out of our sky! Get out—

On the stage, the little figure clutched at the mast and turned slowly, looking out at the roaring mass of voices and fists. His face was blank, except for a small black O *where his mouth should have been. The words of the chant seemed to drive him back like blows, until he was standing only with the greatest effort. The mast that he had been attacking only a moment ago was now his sole support, and it seemed that in a moment even that would fail him. Not that he would lose his grip and fall – no; but that the mast itself would break before he would, and as he stood clinging to the stub, the whole vast pavilion would come down in smothering square miles of stiff brocade, bringing the heavens with it. It was not holding him up. He was holding it up.*

The chant began to falter. The man's head was resting

against the ridgepole, rocking a little as though every shout was a slap. His whole body was doing a dance of torture, and yet at the same time it did not seem to be moving. A horrified Ahhhhh! *rose into the middle of the chant and broke its rhythm; it died away rapidly. In the silence, someone began to weep.*

The young couple sat down, clinging to each other. They had not yet heard one intelligible word from the man on the platform, but he had already wrung them dry – a man that each of them had known intimately since childhood, yet now a man that neither of them had ever seen before. He straightened himself against the ridgepole with great effort, and the pole seemed to stiffen with him. He came forward with slow painful steps, lifted his faraway face – and looked directly into their eyes.

In the intent hush, his familiar voice came soaring to them, as though it had been meant for no one else.

'Children,' he said. 'Children of the cities who have come to the tent; children of the fields and jungles who have come to the tent; children of the seas and nations who have come to the tent; children of the world, children of Home who have come to this tent, listen! There is still time.'

The young man and his bride tightened their grips upon each other's hands; they were frozen to their seats. Though the man on the platform had once been as close to them as blood can tie, he was now something else – and more than a man.

'There is still time,' he said. 'Here is where we and the grass grow up like music.'

The congregation listened.

I

The sea at red noon glared and glided from the hull of the recon cruiser to the horizon on every side. The red sun looked directly down on the deck from the zenith, colouring everything but each man's immediate shadow, the one of the three that the ancients had called the Soul. It made it seem as though the cruiser were forging through a fog of blood.

The second shadow, the Mind, stretched out along the deck, very blurred along the edges. It was being cast by the glittering mass of star-fire at the northern horizon – the great cluster of stars of which this whole system was a marginal member. The third shadow, the Breath, was as usual sharper but dimmer than the Mind, for the white sun which cast it, now thirty degrees above the horizon in the west, was less brilliant than the star cluster. Both, like the soul and everything else, were tinged by the red sun.

And in a moment, the Breath would die. The white sun was about to go out.

The recon boat continued to skim over the sea, the jet engine mounted over its stern howling despite its ring-mounted silencer. The weather was clear, although a black line along the western horizon indicated that it might not stay clear for long. There was, of course, no land in sight. The sea on this side of the world, the side that faced towards the twin planet of Rathe, was empty except for a few insignificant atolls – a whole hemisphere of desert, rolling water.

On Rathe, the emissary Margent had said, they had been looking down on that vast unbroken sea with dry throats for millennia. Rathe was mostly sand.

Aidregh looked up into the flaming sky again, but there was no sign of Rathe now. The air seemed as empty of the twin planet as it was in fact on the other side of Aidregh's world. But it was up there, all right – a planet seven thousand miles in diameter, almost exactly the same size as this one, and only two hundred fifty thousand miles away. The two planets revolved around a common centre, which in turn trailed beyond the red sun in the same orbit at a distance of sixty degrees, all three travelling around the white sun – the Trojan relationship so common in planetary systems, though it had only recently been understood.

Rathe was there, all right. It was invisible now only because it was approaching one of its semi-annual total eclipses of the white sun, the eclipse that the recon craft had travelled so far from home to watch.

Aidregh had seen Rathe earlier in the trip, the first time he had seen it directly, and the memory was still capable of provoking the most powerful, the most baffling complex and ambiguous emotions. It did not matter, really, that he could not see the planet now. There was nothing he had to do but watch the team from his home continent of Thrennen setting up their instruments for the eclipse. As first minister of Thrennen, the largest of all the land-masses and, he hoped, the most powerful, almost his every waking thought these days dealt with Rathe in one way or another. But now, while he was actually under the brow of that far-too-close planet, he was largely useless.

How had the sight of Rathe impressed the very first mariners to cross the meridian between the occupied hemisphere and this one? Of course in a sense every explorer to cross that imaginary boundary line had been the 'first' up to a century ago, since none of them up to then had come back; each new expedition had started with better equipment than the last, but in essentially the same ignorance. They all had expected to find some landfall on the other side of the world; it took a long time to discover that there was nothing there but nearly unbroken water.

The uniform disappearance of all the sailors had given the antipodes an evil name. The invention of the turbine had finally made a Great Circle crossing of the sea possible, but for a while no one had volunteered to try it. No one until Clian.

That had been an epic voyage. Clian had gone out from the harbour of Drash, Thrennen's major port, with a fleet of four crude turbo-powered hulks and some equally crude orders: to bring back pearls, capture a demon or two, and establish the latitude and longitude of the Isle of the Dead. It had been a venture typical of its era in its mixture of daring, engineering, and sheer superstition; a great age, on the whole, and one that Aidregh sometimes wished he had lived in.

Clian had come back with nothing. Nothing but decimated, half-starved crews, a tale of an ocean without one island to break its storm-rolling surface—

. . . And a stone to rest upon the neck of the world, forever after.

Every school child knew that part of his log verbatim. It ran:

Wherefor the further wee went onne – our victual descreasing, and the muggie vapours breed'g grate faintnesse – mor hourlie rose ther out of the sea a Licht such as nonne hadde seen ever befor; till – for wee were now in one hundred thirty-five degrees – then stood reveal'd above the rimme of the water a marvelle as large as the white sonne, though not so bricht, ne mor brilliante than the red. And now were wee al becalm'd, so that wee did drift to and fro, and I order'd the turbine-wheels be fir'd; but even ere this was done, wee saw with grate wonder that yon crescented globe moved not in the skye sithen wee moved, remain'g otherways hung silent above the waters. And as wee moved again, mor violentlie than before because of our need, so arose this marvelle mor quickly in the sky, as tho' it were pois'd eternallie o'er some spotte magickal upon the waters.

Now wee hadde most need of crafte and art, didde both slip mor slylie from us; for that the shippes of captain Dro and captain Fieze hadde spent alle theyre provisionnes; so as wee wer brought into despaire and discomfortte, hadde wee not pleaded with alle the compagnie it was butt one dayes werke more to touch some strande, where alle our wants and woes would be reliev'd; yet if wee return'd to Drash, then should wee be greeted with contumilie, didde wee not starve bie the waye; thus wee hadde grate fortune in maintain'g our travelles.

Yet alway as wee cross'd that sea didde the crescented globe rise o'er our heddes, chang'g in'ts aspecktes fourteen dayes longe, and vanish'g an other fourteen, but alle wayes o'er that same spotte magickal whene'er wee might descrie it. And of alle its appearancies, was its colour moste gloumie, in that it chaung'd from redde to argent continuallie, and was alle of blud-colour ere it didde vanish . . .

The howling of the jet dropped abruptly and died, breaking into Aidregh's reverie. The recon craft lost speed, falling away from its nose-high planing on its hull-step, back into cruising position. They were approaching the path of totality. The sea looked the same as ever, but the astronomers were settling almost grimly to their instruments, with an occasional apprehensive side-glance at the developing storm in the west.

Almost as if in mimicry of the recon craft, a squid almost a foot long broke through the oily surface of the water, its two webbed tentacles stretched tautly into glistening aerofoils, discharging its jet. Seconds later, a dolphin leaped furiously after it, but fell short. A second leap was closer, but the squid, its jet exhausted now, banked to the right sharply and continued to glide; the dolphin's next leap was far off course. The squid continued to glide for nearly a hundred yards before it fell back into the water – and even that might not prove to be far enough, for dolphins travel in schools.

'Useless, isn't it?'

Aidregh started and turned, and then had to fight down an impulse to bare his teeth. There was nothing in Signath's appearance, he reminded himself, to inspire any revulsion. The Opposition party's tribune had a jaw which jutted no more and no less than that of most Thrennen men, or those of the other continent of Noone, for that matter; he had six fingers on each hand like everybody else, including the usual two thumbs; if one took his sandals off, he would be found to have neither more nor less vestigial webbing between his toes than Aidregh or his son Aidresne – or Corlant, his prospective daughter-in-law. Compared to the men of Rathe, whose foggy images Aidregh had been looking at for nearly a year now via television, Signath would have to be accounted a beauty.

Unfortunately, he was mad, in Aidregh's opinion.

'No, don't think it's useless,' Aidregh said carefully. 'The more we know about the geography of Rathe, the better. And we've never had a chance to photograph it before in the special lighting of an eclipse.'

'Photographs!' Signath said. 'In my opinion, we ought to stop photographing and start acting. We know there's going to be war between them and us sooner or later. You can appease them just so long, Aidregh. Why give them the chance to strike the first blow?'

'They don't seem disposed to strike any blows at all,' Aidregh said. 'And it would be just as well *not* to start shaking our fists at them while your party is cutting the guts out of our military budget.'

'You're soft on them, that's all. They don't understand

any language but force. It was you that got us into this alliance with Noone in the first place, and now you've been talking to those Rathemen so long that you've begun to think like they do. We'll put a stop to it when we get control, you can be sure of that.'

'Well, we couldn't very well treat with Rathe if the Noonemen were pulling against us,' Aidregh began. But he no longer expected it to penetrate. The part of the populace that Signath's party represented had no use for that kind of reasoning; it would be impolitic for Signath to pay any attention to it, whatever impression it made on him personally. 'Look,' Aidregh said instead. 'We really know very little about Rathe yet. Isn't it sensible to reserve judgment until we have more facts? And to do our best in the meantime to get the facts?'

No, that wasn't going to work either. Why was it that reservation of judgment, the strongest of all arguments, always sounded like the weakest? And how did you make it prevail against hotheads like Signath?

But Signath was already looking up. He had forgotten Aidregh completely. His teeth were slightly bared, and the shadows on his face were shifting very gradually, turning it prominence by prominence by prominence into the phantom of a skull, as though the darkness were penetrating his taut flesh and transforming it into a vapour. On the deck, his Breath-shadow blurred beside Aidregh's.

The eclipse was beginning. It would last more than an hour.

The solid black edge of Rathe cut its way steadily into the white glare of the primary sun. The now-resting recon craft sidled this way and that in the quiet waves, its deck held in the horizontal plane by the thin and distant hum of its gyroscopes. The instruments shouted skywards with inhumanly still watchfulness.

Steadily, Rathe spread its darkness over the sea. Aidregh found that despite himself he was gulping for air.

At totality, the white sun was gone except for its far-flung atmosphere, and Rathe was illuminated brilliantly on one side by the glare of the star cluster, more faintly on the other by the red sun. Between the two layers of light was a thin, spindle-shaped band of absolute blackness. The instruments began to click, nibbling with invisible mandibles at the world in the sky.

Aidregh shaded and strained his eyes, but somehow the suddenly revealed planet looked less real to him than it had seemed on the photographs. The parti-coloured pattern was partly responsible; it destroyed the illusion of roundness. In addition, the brightness of the sky, and of the white sun's pearly, shimmering corona, made it impossible to pick out fine details on Rathe itself.

There was nothing to see on the planet by the naked eye but the usual white, leprous patches of desert. There were a few oases and isthmuses of green in the quarter-sphere lit by the star cluster. In the area lit by the red sun there was a bright pinpoint of light – could that be a city? No; it was the reflection of the red sun from Rathe's one known small body of water, that is, the only body of water on *this* side of Rathe.

The whole planet was surrounded by still another bright ring which was Rathe's shallow atmosphere, transmitting the light of the white sun so fiercely as to make Rathe's actual perimeter impossible to see. Aidregh wondered how the instruments could possibly mask out that glare, but the astronomers presumably had already anticipated it. Just after the moment of totality, the whole of Rathe was consumed in the bright glare, as if in the attempt to devour the white sun it had itself been devoured instead.

Is that a prophecy? Aidregh thought. And, if it is, does it apply to Rathe – or to us?

A low rumble rolled over the craft from the west. The storm was getting closer.

II

The recon craft volplaned back towards the line as though pursued by the demons Clian had been sent out to capture. The scientists had all disappeared into their respective dark-rooms and cubbies. Most of the diplomatic observers and tribunes were making small talk in the gangways, trying to evade each other's watchfulness long enough to sneak below for some first crumb of new information. The one man who had succeeded in ducking below decks thus far had been almost literally blown back up the ladder, on the updraft of an indignant roar about fogged plates.

Aidregh, who had been dealing with scientists almost daily since he had been given his minister's portfolio, knew well enough that nothing coherent was likely to emerge from the new data for at least several days. Even thereafter it would be a breach of security to discuss the new findings. Thrennen and Noone were still not above trying to jockey for position among the smaller island nations and the Archipelago, even with Rathe hanging above both their heads, even after centuries of inter-island warfare.

As for Aidregh, he had made up his mind not to look at a single film or figure until he was back in his office. There were too many Thrennen tribunes like Signath who were waiting to catch him in some small act which might be for the good of the whole planet, instead of good for Thrennen and to the Isle with foreigners.

And if Signath were given enough rope, he might himself

be caught breaching security – and good riddance. It had been his party, after all, that had attached the gyves of those same security regulations to every possible diplomatic contact with Rathe.

Instead, Aidregh went aft to the cabin of Dr Ni, the physician attached to the expedition, an old friend – and soon-to-be relative, through the marriage of their children. The man was a paradox whose mysteries had always provided a welcome relief from the constant grinding of Aidregh's official cares: erudite far beyond the boundaries of his specialty, especially in history, yet curiously detached towards the momentous age in which he was actually living; hardly past middle age, yet obviously a man of wide experience in all of human living, seemingly already to the point of boredom; a naval officer, but one who regarded all the armed services with the attitude he might have shown towards an especially elaborate game.

Thus Aidregh was not much surprised to find him out of uniform, swinging comfortably in his hammock reading a book. He could not possibly have been on deck during the eclipse, as had every other able-bodied man off duty.

'Hello, Aidregh. Come in; have a drink.'

'Thanks. Obviously you've been here quite a while. What kept you away from the eclipse?'

Dr Ni grinned and held up the book. Aidregh could just make out the title: it was the 'Medani Ballads', a volume the physician must have read twenty times over; he could quote from it verbatim, and often did.

'I don't understand you,' Aidregh said. 'I should think that you of all people would have at least a little curiosity about it – as a scientific man as well as an amateur of history.'

'I've seen it once before,' Dr Ni said, performing at the same time the difficult trick of shrugging gracefully in a hammock. 'As a non-specialist, I could hardly expect to learn anything new from a second look. Besides, Aidregh, sciences differ. There's no more reason why I should be interested in an eclipse than that the astronomical boys should be fascinated by agglutinogens.'

'Surely there's more to it than that. Rathe isn't just a light in the sky, it's a whole inhabited world – and one that may hold your life in its hand.'

'When a man mixes his metaphors that freely,' Dr Ni said, grinning again, 'I'm inclined to doubt that he's thinking very straight. And for that matter, Aidregh, you hold my life in your hand too, don't you? Which menaces me more – a planet a quarter of a million miles away, or a First Minister of Thrennen with his head in a muddle?'

'All right, Ni, suppose you tell me what I ought to be thinking. I don't pretend that I've got more than a marginal understanding of how to deal with Rathe, or what all the implications are – and how the Opposition howls for my head when I don't snap up their easy answers! All I know is that we'll die if the matter isn't handled absolutely flawlessly. Margent isn't giving away any figures, but he's made no secret of the fact that his people have a *large* supply of fission bombs all ready to dump on us if it ever comes to war. I'll listen to advice from anybody – literally anybody.'

'My compliments to you, too,' Ni said wryly. 'I suppose I had that coming. Frankly, Aidregh, I think it *is* going to come to war, and I don't think you can do any more to prevent it than I can. Maybe you can postpone it a little, where I couldn't even do that much. Even so, I wouldn't give you a fish for the life-span of the next generation.'

'That's Corlant you're talking about, you know.'

'I'm talking about my daughter,' Ni said, unruffled, 'and your son, and the whole population of this planet. The discovery of Rathe came either too soon or too late for us,

Aidregh. For survival's sake, we should either have discovered it back in prehistory somewhere, so we'd be used to its presence by now, or several centuries in the future, when – I say this doubtfully – we'd be more rational.'

'You sound rational enough to me,' Aidregh said gloomily.

'That doesn't mean a thing. There are large numbers of rational men in Thrennen, and Noone too, otherwise we couldn't have made the alliance, shaky though it seems to be. But it's the popular feeling that's going to decide the matter in the end – and you know what that is.'

The old, old depression began to flood back upon Aidregh full force. He knew. He had himself felt a faint thread of that superstitious horror back there on deck, while he had watched the Breath-shadow destroyed by the thing in the sky.

'They think that Rathe has no business being up there in *their* sky,' he said. 'And it means nothing to them that less than one per cent of them will ever see Rathe at all. Or that all this expanse of ocean might just as well not be here at all, for all the difference it makes in their lives.'

'Since it's no good to them, they're determined that it shall do them evil,' Ni said. 'That's about the way it goes. We're in a scientific age, more or less, Aidregh, but it takes a situation like this to reveal how few people actually are living in it, with their minds as well as their bodies. Do you know that in Clian's time, the percentage of people who believed in astrology was *smaller* than it is now? Nine out of every ten patients I have won't step out on the street when Rathe is occulting their birth constellation, or lining up with some of the outer planets in some stupid configuration or other. And most of the time, the astrologer they consult is giving them just any old figures at all – *he* knows that they won't be able to check on the actual position of Rathe at that time. He knows that they wouldn't check it if the planet were right over their heads, let alone being on the other side of the world all the time!'

Aidregh said nothing. Nine out of ten! And most of Ni's patients were high brass, and/or civilian government officials. Of course the figure was probably somewhat exaggerated, but still . . .

'I'll tell you a dilly,' Ni added conversationally. 'You know the new planet that was discovered last year – the fifth one, counting our pair as one – that colossal gas giant, I've forgotten its name. Well, the astrologers have decided that it controls the monorail lines! And it does no good to ask what it was controlling before there were any monorail lines; it hadn't been discovered then, so it didn't exist. And yet the thing's one hundred ten thousand miles in diameter, and one of its moons is as big as the whole planet of Nesmet – the so-called War Planet! Wait'll the boys get to work on that satellite, *then* we'll see some champion rationalizations. It may turn out to have been influencing popular dancing all this time!'

The planet Ni was talking about was Herak, of course. It was eight billion five hundred million miles from the white sun, had fourteen satellites at last reports, had an orbital period of two hundred sixty-five years . . . The figures fell into place automatically. To be First Minister these days required an extensive knowledge of descriptive astronomy – a knowledge that had to be kept concealed from the public, because it might lead people to think that spaceflight to the other planets was nearer than they had been led to believe, and that might make them wonder which planet was being visited, and that might lead them to conclude that naturally it would be the nearest one except Rathe, and that might lead them to think that there was an expedition on Nesmet right now, and the word might get back to Rathe, somehow . . .

And right at the moment, the Nesmet expedition was overdue, which meant that it would be eighty-one days before Nesmet would again be in a position which would allow a take-off for home.

Officially, the first manned spaceflight was yet to be made. The public knew only that an orbital satellite had been successfully put into position six years ago, for the ostensible purpose of serving as a television relay station. Informed amateurs had immediately concluded that no such station was needed for the short distances over which television had to operate on the island continents, and correctly assumed that the satellite was there to communicate with Rathe. There had been an Isle of a stink about that; it had been quietened only by the government's assurance that the station was also *watching* Rathe, a never-sleeping sentinel and scout.

Since that series of guesses had hit home, no further word had been said about spaceflight except that Progress was Being Made. The succeeding events had been even more frightening in their possibilities for sensation. There had been, for instance, the unmanned missile which had been supposed to circle Rathe, take pictures, and come home again. Margent had reported, quite politely, that the Rathemen had shot it down. Furthermore, Margent had added in moderate tones, anything that approached Rathe henceforth would have to give advance warning, and would not be allowed to return home before landing at a designated spot on Rathe for a careful inspection.

In short – although Margent did not say so – the Rathemen knew that the terrain on the other side of Rathe had always been invisible to the sister planet, and they meant to protect that invisibility for a while. Shortly thereafter, Aidregh's own world had had a similar visitor, and had sent a similar message back. Attempts by both sides to send missiles outside the range of detection, or at least of feasible anti-missile action, apparently had come to identical bad ends; at least Aidregh knew that there was still no picture of the far side of Rathe in *his* files. What pictures were in Margent's files could only be guessed, but Aidregh was reasonably sure that if any existed, they were all pretty bad. The weather on his own wet world wasn't as cooperative to cameras as was the clear desert air of Rathe.

If only the Nesmet expedition hadn't been forced to keep radio silence—

He looked up with a start of embarrassment. Dr Ni had resumed reading his book, but he put it down again at Aidregh's movement.

'I expect,' he said, 'something brilliant in response, after all that cogitation.'

'I'm sorry, Ni. I got sidetracked. I don't even remember what you said last. I'm not very good company these days, I'm afraid.'

'I don't mind being quiet while a man thinks. But you need practice at thinking about something else. You're worrying yourself into hysteria. Don't deny it – I'm a doctor, I can see the signs. Got any hobbies, Aidregh?'

'Hobbies? Oh, I guess Aidresne is about the only hobby I—'

'No, no,' Dr Ni said, frowning. 'You're not the man to be relaxed by your family. Aidresne's a fine boy, but I mean some interest you don't *worry* about. Do you like music?'

'I'm tune-deaf, I'm afraid.'

'I wish our schools recognized that as a serious physical handicap, as serious as being minus a leg, and gave compensating training; but they don't, so that's that. How about reading? Like this?' He waved the 'Medani Ballads'.

'I haven't much time for reading. Of course in school I—'

'Oh, school. Poetry is for adults, not children. Here, try this.'

He riffled through the volume for a brief moment, and then read:

> 'Hopeful of poetry, the nearsighted heart
> Puts to the moment's pain a burning-glass;
> The soft bruise bleeds, and mourns fatality,
> Weeping, This does not pass.
>
> 'Weeping is bitter, but tragedy in tears
> Lies taut and salty on the drying cheek.
> The past is sand. Beside the clock
> Even the heart is weak.
>
> 'Quietly the ducts of pain are emptied,
> Frayed in converse with the smiling shears.
> There is no rain but rain, nor better
> Aegis than the umbrella of the years.'

'It's . . . interesting,' Aidregh said hesitantly. 'I'm not sure I understood it all. He says that . . . that *This too shall pass away*, isn't that it?'

'Yes, but there's more to it than that. He says that to lose even the immediate impact of a sorrow is to lose something valuable – as serious a loss as forgetting the sharpness of a joy. They were wise people, the Medani. It was Thrennen that wiped them out, wasn't it?'

'I think it was.' A brief ghost moved across Aidregh's forebrain: the shadow of his wife, dead before she had heard Aidresne's first cry. Dr Ni, who had been the attending physician, had said that death in childbirth was not always preventable, even now. The marriage, late for Aidregh, had been a political one, but he had learned to love the quiet

Noone girl. In the instant of the passage of the shadow, Rathe seemed of no importance whatsoever.

Then it was gone.

He shook himself. 'I don't think it's for me, Ni. It's . . . depressing. I've got enough to depress me as it is.'

'But it's none of it yours, my friend. You need something to remind you of yourself once in a while – of the things that are important to you as a person. You're killing yourself in the name of a set of abstractions.'

'Well,' Aidregh said, rising, 'that's what I'm being paid to do.'

III

The ship made its first stop in the Archipelago, to drop off the scientists who had come from there; the Archipelago was highly important politically, for it represented the balance of power between Thrennen and Noone. Aidregh left the ship and caught a plane out of Bros Airport for Drash.

Dr Ni refused to join him; he said he was enjoying the cruise. Aidregh did not press him, though he could not help wondering what was so novel about a cruise to a naval officer.

The plane's pilot succeeded inadvertently in deepening Aidregh's gloom by approaching Drash from the side of Thrennen looking towards the empty ocean on the other side of the world, thus passing directly over an irregular patch of concrete set into the ground near the coast. The patch, several square miles in area, was studded with shallow concrete boxes, next to each of which was a small spot of shadow.

There were very few people in the world who knew what the patch was, but Aidregh knew well enough. The spots of shadow were the removable roofs of long concrete-lined tubes, each a hundred feet in diameter and leading deep into the earth. Steel guide-rails ran along the walls of the tubes, and at the bottom of each tube, on the rails, there rested an enormous guided missile, many of them already armed with their thermonuclear warheads. The concrete stubs visible from the plane were the tops of cubical control chambers set into the ground.

Rather complete intelligence reports indicated that there was another such battery on Noone, even larger than Thrennen's. Aidregh did not know how Noone's missiles were armed, and the Noonemen weren't talking, but there had been several test fusion explosions in Noone a few years ago. There didn't seem to be much doubt.

Nor could there be any doubt that there were such firing plazas on Rathe. That the Rathemen's weapons were nuclear rather than thermonuclear made no practical difference, considering the relative smallness of the targets on Aidregh's world; atomic bombs would be more than sufficient.

The two planets were circling each other like duellists with their knives at each other's throats.

Then the concrete patch had vanished behind the plane, and they were coming in over Drash – once a hide-hut village situated at the mouth of the biggest river which emptied into the sea on the western side of Thrennen, but nearly a thousand years of alluvial deposits had done their work; now the nearest water was a mile away along a broad shelving beach. As seen from the air, the buildings of the city looked like so many parallelograms, ranging from thirty to a hundred and fifty feet square; their concrete roofs were only very slightly pitched, to allow for drainage of the frequent rains. The buildings were set wide apart, and Thrennen's lush vegetation hid the concrete paving that connected them, as the roofs themselves hid the massive concrete pillars that supported them, and the walls of lignin-impregnated plywood with their large oblong windows.

Noonemen commonly sneered at Thrennen architecture, which they said looked as if it had never left the blueprint stage, but Aidregh found it soothing; after all, it was home. He was obscurely glad to be back; the eclipse had unsettled him much more than he liked to admit, even to himself.

He went directly to his office and rang for Aidresne, who according to custom served as his aide. While he waited, he shuffled through the carefully-screened stack of papers left on his lectern as requiring his immediate attention. It was for once not a very big stack; the eclipse had conveniently scheduled itself while the Tribunal was not in session, so there were no bills to read. The political summary, prepared by the secretary-general of Aidregh's party, showed the situation getting worse at about its usual speed: too fast. The Opposition was gaining ground; even in Signath's absence, the populace was getting steadily more war-minded, and something similar was going on in Noone. It was perfectly possible, though not yet predictable, that a war with Rathe would have to be undertaken, as the only means of preventing the two islands from destroying each other – a 'cure' precisely comparable to shooting the patient, but that appeared to be what was at the back of Signath's mind all the same. The Cluster only knew what inflammatory speeches he was cooking up right now, out of whatever he thought he had seen from the recon cruiser.

With a sigh, Aidregh opened the small cooking machine to see what the staff had sent him as a welcome-home meal, though he was, in fact, not very hungry. It proved to be roast tapir, a favourite of his, with three cultivated vegetables and two wild ones, all on the three 'mechanical' plates which were the traditional service of the First Minister: one showing a sea-going vessel like Clian's, one a primitive aircraft with a stern-mounted jet, and one a rocket as thin as a stylus. That last had been Aidregh's own addition; each new

Minister was expected to add one plate and retire one, as a symbol of the progress achieved under his ministry. The borders of the plates were formalized wreaths of triolets, the flower of Thrennen, arranged in recurrent groups of four.

Our architecture may not be very imaginative, Aidregh thought, but in ceramics nobody beats Thrennen for grace of design, or fine workmanship either. Feeling obscurely better, he fell to.

'Welcome back, Father.'

Aidregh turned from his meal with a smile. Aidresne's close-cropped stubble of hair was black, which put him in a minority among the generally fair men of Thrennen; he had of course inherited it from his mother. He was a stocky youngster, somewhat shorter than Aidregh, and his father had never considered him handsome. (Luckily, Corlant disagreed.) But he was thoughtful and quick, which meant a good deal more.

'Glad to see you, Aidresne. I want you to take charge of the eclipse reports as soon as they come in – they'll be here in only a day or so – and prepare a summary for me. Unless they're overwhelmingly important, I don't want details; give me a weighted summary, together with any opinions the military may see fit to offer. But I want that military assessment *boiled*; you know how long-winded these generals can be.'

'All right,' Aidresne said. 'I hope it'll be worth the work. Did much come of it, do you think?'

'Hard to say. I can't believe that the Rathemen would put up any key installations where we could see them. Any important structures that are on our side of Rathe would be likely to be obsolete – put up while the Rathemen still thought our planet uninhabited.'

'That would be pretty obsolete, all right,' Aidresne said judiciously. 'By about five hundred years, I'd guess.'

'You're exaggerating. They may have decided the planet was *habitable* as far back as all that, but they didn't know for sure that we were here until we discovered radio. Anyhow a century is as good as a millennium when it's military obsolescence you're talking about. How's Corlant?'

'She's just the same,' the boy said, smiling faintly. 'Wonderful.'

'Good. I must say your prospective father-in-law takes a very dim view of your future, and everybody else's for that matter.'

'So do I,' Aidresne said slowly. 'But I can still hope. I think Dr Ni has forgotten how to do that, or at least he's out of practice.'

'Well, I'm still hoping, too. I've got to. Any word from Nesmet?'

'Nothing at all. The planet's on its way back into opposition with us, though, and the astronomers at the satellite are watching for any signs of activity. What they expect to see is beyond me. I can't believe myself that Captain Arpen will attempt any take-off until the moment of closest approach; sixty million miles is plenty far enough to travel.'

'It's more than that,' Aidregh reminded him. 'That's only the difference between our distance from the primary and Nesmet's. Don't forget that Nesmet's orbit is tilted eighty-seven degrees to ours. That lengthens the trip by more than a third again.' He leaned one elbow on the lectern and put his chin sombrely into his hand. 'As a matter of fact, we weren't ready to undertake anything so grandiose, not by many years. We only pushed ourselves into it because of Rathe. I'll be quite stunned if that expedition gets back at all, Aidresne, though don't tell *anyone* I said so.'

Both men were silent for a long moment. Then Aidregh sighed.

'Everything depends on Rathe, as usual,' he said. 'I suppose we'd better try to talk to Margent again.'

Aidresne shrugged and opened the door. They went out together, arm in arm, father and son. There was still that in a shaky world.

The communications centre, like everything else dealing with Rathe, was secret; even the small underground monorail line which led to it from the capitol was known to comparatively few people. Of course, communicating with Rathe, via the orbital station, was only a small part of its function. It also received planet-wide weather reports, astronomical, physical, and medical research data, and navigation information from the station, and funnelled them out all over the planet. Since the treaty with Noone, the orbital station was no longer strictly a Thrennen enterprise, and the size of the centre duly reflected that.

Most of the centre's complement affected not to recognize their First Minister and his son at all; this was protocol, although most of the men were so busy that it was possible they never saw Aidregh and Aidresne anyhow. A staffer took them directly to the small air-conditioned chamber used by the high brass to receive important communications direct, as they came in. It was sparsely furnished: a few couches, a few lecterns, a small cubby for refreshments – and three television screens.

Aidresne sat down and waited matter-of-factly, but Aidregh picked out a lectern; he was too tense to sit, and in any event had always preferred to work standing. This was going to be work. After several moments, the central screen lit, swirled and steadied.

Margent was looking at them.

It was as difficult as usual to see exactly what Margent looked like, for he was swathed and hooded as always, with the many robes and capes which the Rathemen wore against the savage extremes of heat and cold through which thin-aired Rathe passed daily. The face that looked out of the screen was roughly like Aidregh's own; that is, it possessed the same organs in the same number and in about the same relationship to each other; but there were a good many small differences.

The Ratheman's eyebrows, for example, although they were dark and fierce, were not mounted on a bony prominence as Aidregh's were. His nose was not flat, and the nostrils, so small as to be almost invisible, pointed straight down; on either side of his nose were two small pits whose sensory function was unknown. His mouth was perhaps half the length of Aidregh's, and his chin did not jut forward at all, but was small and sharply pointed. All these, taken together with a forehead that was just as broad and even higher than Aidregh's, made the face inside the hood seem almost triangular.

The rest was conjecture, put together by scientists working partly from hints that Margent had let drop, partly from occasional glimpses caught under the folds of the robes, partly from the obvious terrain and meteorology of Rathe itself. The Rathemen's hands were six-fingered like their own – and so they, too, had worked out a duodecimal numbering system – but longer and more slender. Their bodies were slight, lean and tough, with skins like fine leather, but they were almost uniformly taller than Aidregh's race.

They were without doubt mammals, with two sexes, like Aidregh's people, but nowadays Aidregh found himself thinking of neither race in those terms. Obscurely, Margent made him feel as though Aidregh represented a species which had evolved directly from frogs, while the Rathemen seemed like a race of supremely intelligent lizards. It was absurd, but it symbolized the sum of the differences Aidregh sensed between Margent and himself.

'We trust you had good seeing,' Margent said in his dry, whispery voice. He spoke excellent Thrennen; Aidregh understood Rathe – the planet had only one language – but comparatively imperfectly.

'Very good,' Aidregh said noncommittally. In the 1·344 seconds it would take the microwaves carrying his voice and image to cross the gulf to Rathe, and the identical lapse that would be imposed on whatever Margent said next, he found time to wonder whether the opening gambit had been meant as irony. Margent was referring to the eclipse, of course; but surely he also knew that the seeing all over Aidregh's world was infernally poor at best.

Margent, however, dropped the matter. 'We believe that it is time we treated with each other directly,' he said. 'There are high matters coming to a head among my people which will not allow of long postponement.'

'By all means,' Aidregh said sincerely, but feeling the invisible hand of caution always on his shoulder. 'Negotiation is obviously the only way out of the situation in which we find ourselves. Properly, our two worlds should be as bound together by trade and open intercourse as they are by gravity; it is the only civilized way.'

'So I have long maintained,' Margent said gravely. 'But my thoughts cannot be my own here; they are composite thoughts, representing, in some part, attitudes to which Margent as a person cannot subscribe. Your situation is the same, I believe.'

'It is indeed,' Aidregh said feelingly. 'But if you and I can come to any sort of reasonable agreement, I think I can control the dissident elements among my people – or, at least, nullify any hostile action they may advocate.'

The time lag seemed interminable. Margent had almost completely taken him aback. Usually the Ratheman was involved, subtle and indirect in everything he said.

'That is also true with me,' Margent said. 'But I cannot do it without direct contact; it is the price the religious among my people demand. When may I expect you, then?'

Behind him, Aidregh heard his son gasp. Evidently Aidresne, too, had not got the point until now; in their startlement at Margent's new directness, they had not spotted the still-present thread of indirection.

And the question was dynamite. A personal visit to Rathe now, however greatly the notion tempted Aidregh, would puzzle and disturb half the population, and – without more than a few prods in the right direction by Signath and the Opposition – it would absolutely inflame the other half. Altogether, it would do not a particle of good, for any agreements he might make with Margent as a result of it would be without force; Aidregh's government would not outlast the initial journey.

'I misunderstood you,' Aidregh said at last. 'Is this present contact not direct enough? The beam between us is reasonably tight, I am told.'

'The matters of which I speak cannot be discussed in this fashion,' Margent said. 'They are religious. I would not be permitted to broadcast them in any form. Personal contact is essential.'

Religious? But it would do no good to ask Margent what he meant by that; he had, after all, just given his only answer to such a question: he could not discuss it.

'I see,' Aidregh said. 'Nevertheless, Margent, you find me reluctant for good reasons. There are State matters which demand my presence here; were I to leave now, I would lose control over my dissident people, and that control is essential to the survival of both planets. I speak bluntly; surely you can see the force of the argument?'

'I see it,' Margent said. 'But let me remind you that I, too, am in that same sense helpless. You must come. I assure you solemnly that nothing else will prevent war between our worlds in the long run.'

The air hung heavily in the room. Perhaps – even probably – Margent had not meant that to be taken as a threat; to him it seemed a simple statement of fact. But a threat was what it was – the ultimate threat. With a dolorous heart, Aidregh looked to Aidresne.

His son said quietly, 'We had better go.'

'Very well,' Aidregh said, turning back to the invisible cameras and the screens. 'It will be a great adventure for me, if nothing else. But you, too, must yield in some measure to the situation here, Margent. It will be utterly impossible for me to come at once. I cannot even name a date now. How long can you postpone your crisis, whatever it is?'

'How soon can you come?' Margent said.

Aidregh drew a deep breath. 'No sooner than a year from now.'

Margent seemed to think about it a long time, but the tension had so distorted Aidregh's sense of duration that it might have been only the 1·344-second lag. At last he said:

'I can undertake that postponement. In the meantime I will be unable to talk to you. It is known here that we now have nothing else to talk about, except this one matter. Farewell.'

Upon the word, the screen went dark.

IV

Floating a bill through the Tribunal providing the necessary funds, enough to provide for three ships capable of getting to Rathe and back, did not prove as difficult as Aidregh had anticipated. Publicly, of course, the appropriations bill was labelled only as 'needed for the national defence'; those few tribunes who had to be told why the extra money was needed – including, for reassurances's sake, the President of Noone and the Premier of the Archipelago – were told in strict secrecy that it was for a second attempt on Nesmet.

That did the trick, and the bill went through. After that, Aidregh was able to stop thinking about a journey to Rathe for a while. Most of the time.

The days were certainly full enough; they flew by as stealthily and swiftly as mice. First of all, the results of the eclipse came in, and they turned out to be far better than Aidregh had hoped. Of course the observations that had been made from the surface of the sea did not amount to much, but nobody had really expected that they would. Those that came from the satellite station, however, were full of detail. They added up to an almost complete map of the visible surface of Rathe, as it might have been photographed from a ship cruising only fifty miles above the planet. Every major and minor city was visible; the extent and nature of the deserts accurately charted; bodies of water, all the way down to small lakes, identified; roads mapped— It amounted to a real gold mine of information, much better than anything that had ever been available before.

'This is very good,' he told Aidresne at last, after reading his son's report with prolonged and intense concentration. 'Now we have targets – not only the major cities we already knew about, but smaller communications hubs, water supplies, and so on. And the generals say that this thing that looks like a spider web, here on this photo, is a key supply dump of some kind; the road-patterns leading to it are supposed to make that inarguable.' He sighed. 'If it comes to war, now, we'll be able to leave nothing on the visible face of Rathe but puddles of slag. What a horrible thing to be certain of.'

'That's all very well,' Aidresne said. 'But what bothers me is that we still don't have any data on Rathe's offensive power. Nothing of that kind shows in this material.'

'I know. We didn't expect them to be fools enough to put such things where we could see them. I think we know this much, Aidresne: whatever their striking force is, it's sufficient.'

'But how do we know?' the boy objected. 'Their weapons are only nuclear, and they'll have to shoot more or less blind. Some of us are bound to survive, whereas we know we can sear their visible hemisphere clean – and probably saturate the invisible side, with properly spaced megaton weapons.'

Aidregh shook his head. 'We don't dare lull ourselves with any such notion,' he said. 'They have vastly more land area than we have. Without accurate knowledge of targets, "saturating" the other side of Rathe is only a dream. We'd get complete extermination of the Rathemen only by luck – if that's what we have to mean by "luck" these days – and if they have deep shelters, we wouldn't get it even then. The only sane way of viewing the matter is to assume that war would mean death for both of us; otherwise—'

A buzzer interrupted him. He opened a switch on the lectern, and Dr Ni's voice came from the speaker under it; Ni was, of course, in Drash as a member of the eclipse team.

'Aidregh? News for you. Thought you'd better know right away. Bribed the chance to be the first to tell you.'

'All right, Ni, go ahead.'

'The Nesmet expedition is on its way in. They didn't wait for favourable opposition; they took off as soon as Nesmet rounded the sun on the way back towards us. They've been in flight over a year!'

Aidregh and his son exchanged stunned glances. That could only mean that Captain Arpen had discovered something of overwhelming importance. He would never have taken such a risk for any other reason.

'Go ahead,' Aidregh said tensely.

'They just got in radio contact with Drash fifteen minutes ago, through the satellite station,' Ni's voice said. Even he sounded mildly excited. 'They're about a thousand miles out from the station's orbit now, but on our side of the planet. Arpen waited until Rathe was in our radio shadow before calling us.'

'Of course, those were his orders. When will he touch down?'

'The day after tomorrow. He's dangerously low on fuel, and has to land by the most conservative method; I don't understand the details, of course. But I thought you'd want to know at once.'

'Yes. Thanks.' Aidregh closed the switch with a faint grin. Evidently his old friend was not quite so immune to great events outside medicine as he had pretended to be. But the grin disappeared in a hurry.

'This,' Aidregh said slowly, 'is a prime shock.'

'What can it mean?'

'I wish I knew. All I can say about it now is that it's bad news.'

'Bad news?' Aidresne said. 'How can you know—'

'It's the Rathe expedition I'm thinking of, Aidresne,' he

said impatiently. 'We got the money for it ostensibly to build another Nesmet ship, never forget that. I told Signath and those other idiots that I didn't think Arpen would make it back, and that we shouldn't be caught short if he didn't. I didn't want to tell them any such thing, but after that ultimatum of Margent's, I couldn't do anything else. And now here's Arpen back, and not only back, but something like sixty days before we could possibly have begun to count him lost!'

Aidresne looked at him appraisingly, and a little upsettingly, as though he were seeing his father for the first time.

'I wonder,' he said. 'Father, can you really be hoping that Arpen will still crash?'

'No, no! By the Cluster, Aidresne! You know better than that. We have to find out what's made him take a risk like this. I'm only explaining why this early arrival of his has put us into a political box. It has, that's all. That's all there is to it.'

But Aidresne's suggestion had, for a moment, lighted in him an ugly little flare of hope. He fought it down, grimly.

Captain Arpen got his seared and battered ship down on to Drash Airport as lightly as any falling leaf, with just enough propellant left in its tanks to soak into a medium-large bath sponge. For a landing that was supposed to have been secret, of a flight that no one was supposed to know about, it accumulated a sizeable reception committee even before the ship's hull was cool enough to allow the air locks to open.

Arpen went through the reception committee like a knife through cheese. Though he was haggard with exhaustion, he was equally deaf to all pleas that he and his crew rest for a few days before attempting to report.

'Where's the First Minister?' he kept demanding. 'Osanto, if you drop those film cans I'll . . . all right, all right, just stick close to me and stay awake. Where's the First Minister? Ah! Aidregh, Aidregh! Make these flunkeys let me through! I've got to talk to you where it's quiet. Osanto, get into the Minister's car and pass me those cans. And don't you double-damn dast go to sleep, or you won't wake up for a week. Sir, can't we get the Isle *out* of here? We've been driving for over a year to get this stuff home – Osanto, wake up, the Cluster blast your soul—'

Aidregh issued the necessary orders in a hurry, and the car shot away from the airport. He was completely in awe of this cadaverous young man with the fiercely burning, glassily unblinking eyes. Captain Arpen had, after all, just finished the most epic voyage in human history; and the drive in him even now, when he was within an inch of keeling over, was like the fury of a blast furnace. In the face of it, Aidregh melted away as passively as a trick spoon in hot water.

In the First Minister's office, Captain Arpen and the zombielike Osanto, his observation officer – before the trip the most promising young astronomer in all of Thrennen – spread their photographs and maps indiscriminately all over the carpeted floor. Arpen talked to Aidregh, Aidresne, Dr Ni and two anonymous generals as though he recognized none of them, spilling out the words with machine-pistol velocity between gulps of a hot drink some steward had pressed upon him. His eyes stared like those of a man who has seen a vision. Osanto said nothing and drank nothing; he only pointed drearily at the proper prints when Arpen's orders reached him, across some personal gulf of ultimate weariness.

'We stuck to the dark side of Nesmet all the time, except for a few forays into the twilight zone,' Arpen said. 'Nesmet has a few traces of atmosphere which we didn't expect – heavy gases, and not much of those. The dark side is a wilderness of snow, not real snow of course, but frozen methane and carbon dioxide and other organic gases. Every time one of those snowfields wobbles over into the twilight zone, it evaporates and goes howling off on to the hot side. At the same time, on the other terminator, the atmosphere gets caught in the shadow and freezes out within less than half an hour. There are huge spires of it built up as high as mountains, before you even begin to understand what's going on, but at the next libration it sublimes away again like two million hurricanes. Show them, Osanto.'

Osanto nudged at a photo with his toe; Captain Arpen gulped at his drink.

'It's a miserable place to work,' Arpen said. 'Because of the atmosphere, and the distance, our pictures of the far side of Rathe aren't anything wonderful. But they're not too bad either— Where was I? Oh, the pictures. They pretty well confirm our speculations as to where the main highlands and lowlands should be. And they show several of the major cities. There's one real whopper; can't be anything but the capital of Rathe. They also show that the only major body of water the Rathemen have over there is smaller than the Niabrand Sea on *our* side; one signal fusion bomb would boil it dry. Where's that infra-red shot, Osanto?'

Nudge. Gulp.

'This is wonderful,' Aidregh said. 'It's already more than we'd hoped for. But captain, offhand I don't see anything sensational enough to justify the risk you took. What if you'd not got back at—'

'We got back,' Arpen said fiercely. 'And this is only the beginning. Sir, if you interrupt me at any length, I won't be able to stay awake through it. You can see what shape

Osanto's in, and I'm not in much better, though I'm up to my ear-whorls in amphetamine. Believe me, these pictures we took on Nesmet are nothing. We got a series of thirty-five shots of the back side of Rathe *on the way in*. We tried to use the big telescope that close to home, but of course it didn't work. We lost it, and both men we floated outside with it to man it – one meteor, just one little spec of something and *fft*! nothing but gas. But even from inside the ship, with nothing but the plotting 'scope, the pictures came out better than the Nesmet prints. Show them, Osanto.'

There was no response. Osanto was asleep on his feet, so deeply asleep that he was not even swaying after his long battle with no-gravity, he was tied down to his home planet as contentedly as a mushroom.

'By the Cluster!' Arpen said. 'All right, let him sleep. He's been working like a slave.' The captain went down on his knees like a broken umbrella and began to paw through the pictures himself. At last he heaved himself triumphantly to his feet, weaving visibly with dizziness.

'Here it is,' he said. 'Look at this, sir. Almost as good as a contour map. And here – this regular white patch on the north-east highland. It's camouflaged, but it shows on the infra-red; what do you make of that?'

The generals joined Aidregh in a huddle over the picture, but he did not need them. He had seen a thing just like this some time ago, from the air, near Drash.

'It's an artillery emplacement,' he said slowly. 'A Firing Plaza, like ours – and the one they have in Noone. But bigger.'

'That's what Osanto says,' Arpen said, regaining his balance with a terrible effort. His eyes were half closed. 'Now we know where it is. We could hit it first if we had to. Osanto's picked out four or five smaller ones. He can show them to you. I can't, I don't know the signs.'

'Four or five?' Aidregh whispered. 'Are we as out-gunned as all that?'

'Don't know,' Captain Arpen said drunkenly. He forced his eyelids up again. 'Anyhow, these pictures aren't the reason why we left Nesmet early. We knew we were going to try to get them on the way back home. And we couldn't predict how they'd turn out. We didn't take off until we'd found . . . it was—'

He stopped and looked with awful eyes at Aidregh. 'What was I saying?' he said. 'I was saying something.'

'Something you found on Nesmet, something that sent you home early. Captain Arpen, can't you let it wait until—'

'No,' Arpen said. 'No. Sir, there was a Rathe expedition on Nesmet. That was what I wanted to say. Sir, they beat us to it.'

'Are you sure?' Aidregh whispered.

'No doubt about it. Their camp was pretty well beaten up, but not so much that we couldn't identify it positively. It's theirs. There are remains of still a third observation station on the planet. It isn't ours, and it isn't Rathe's; and it's *much* older, much older. Who could have put it there we don't know. But it gave us weathering and other standards for assessing the age and nature of the Rathe camp. The Rathemen landed on Nesmet a year before we did. Maybe two.'

'Aha,' one of the generals said, as though whatever had occurred to him satisfied him profoundly. 'That means that the Rathemen have pictures of *our* "invisible" hemisphere, too. Very interesting.'

'Yes,' Arpen said. 'I thought it was interesting. That's why I left Nesmet early.' He sighed raggedly. 'There. Are the . . . pictures . . . I brought . . . them . . .' His breathing was broken by a sudden convulsion, and he began to lean.

'Home,' he said. His eyes closed, and he toppled as

though he had been stoned. The strewn photographs fluttered out from under him.

Dr Ni was kneeling beside him in an instant, feeling for his pulse, ausculating his chest. The photographs came to rest in the general litter. The physician raised his head slowly, looking up at Aidregh with a blank and astonished face.

'Why,' Dr Ni said wonderingly, 'he's dead, Aidregh. His heart burst.'

Aidregh could not move. He looked down sorrowfully at the contorted, wasted body – the detritus of a hero. He had never known Captain Arpen well; mixed inextricably into his sorrow was the knowledge that nobody would ever know who had established that third – no, that first! – observatory on Nesmet; nor why. Where could the observers have come from? Surely not from frigid Gao, a planet twice the size of the home planet or Rathe; an enormous four hundred fifty million miles from the white sun, its atmosphere a poisonous mixture of hydrogen, methane and ammonia. Surely not from the next nearest satellite of planetary size, the thirty-nine hundred-mile Herak I, eighty-five thousand millions of miles from the white sun?

What life-form, incredibly different from Aidregh's race *or* the Rathemen, could be still abroad in this wide-flung, cold, perfectly hostile solar system?

They would never know; their time was running out. Neither they nor the Rathemen could bother to do so much as ask the question, let alone hope for an answer.

This was the end of the line. The targets were known, now, on both worlds. When the missiles flew, they would go home unerringly. Arpen had died to make that a fact; and perhaps some Rathemen had died, earlier, for the same cause.

The cause of suicide. That was for Margent to judge, if he

could. There was nothing left for Aidregh now but the expedition to Rathe, far too soon, and for no hope . . . no hope at all. The knives were now more than at the worlds' throats. They were poised above their backs.

V

Maybe I've got no business being First Minister of Thrennen anyhow, Aidregh thought later; every time I think I understand how people are thinking, they show me that I really haven't had the foggiest notion.

For instance: the primary public reaction against the expedition to Rathe, as it turned out, was not political at all. It arose instead from the fact that the trip would postpone the wedding.

The courtship of Corlant and Aidresne had been followed with the greatest avidity by the press almost since its beginning, to the great discomfiture of both of them. Inevitably, and against both their wishes, the marriage ceremony had been planned as a massive State affair, attended by functionaries of both Thrennen parties, as well as by diplomats from every other nation. It had been a generation since Thrennen had seen such a circus of pomp nicely blended with sentimentality, and the public, already fed to the teeth with the constantly overhanging threat of war, had been waiting for this new spectacle with its figurative tongue hanging out.

Nevertheless, postponed the wedding had to be, no matter what the public thought. Aidresne had to go with Aidregh to Rathe, as a matter of course, and there was no way to sweeten the dose; were Aidresne to be left behind, Signath would lose no time in branding the expedition an act of suicide, with Aidresne deliberately left in a position where he could pick up the reins of power and keep the Opposition out of the government. That would be sufficient at least to drum up a recall referendum, which would be weakening no matter who won it. Of course, taking Aidresne along exposed Aidregh's party to the contrary charge that Aidregh was cutting the head off his own government, but that was a weak tack to take with a public that expected the First Minister's son to accompany him on every major political journey, no matter how far away.

Then Corlant was announced.

Aidregh was more than glad to see her, and happily jettisoned his business for the time being. He was quite convinced that she was the loveliest girl he had ever seen in his life, excepting only his wife, and had felt nothing but warm approval of his son's good taste when the engagement had been decided upon. But the expression on her face when she came in sent a stab of misgiving through him. Like all Thrennen women, she lacked the rather prognathous jaw common to the Thrennen male, indeed in Corlant the jaw line was quite rounded; today that plump firm arrowhead was echoed by another arrow cut deeply between her eyebrows. His fears were confirmed by her first words.

'Aidregh,' she said in her low, melodious voice, 'I have a citizen's petition. I want to go to Rathe.'

'I can't let you do that,' Aidregh said gently. 'It's going to be pretty dangerous, Corlant.'

'Captain Arpen made it to Nesmet and back,' she said quietly. 'That's much farther. And the ship he used wasn't as good as the Rathe ships will be – and it wasn't a liveable planet he was going to, with people to help him when he got there.'

'All true,' Aidregh admitted. 'But Arpen's feat was something more than a miracle, Corlant – and even so, it killed him. This trip of ours is still going to be hazardous; we aren't advanced that much in the art of spaceflight. There just hasn't been time to profit by most of Arpen's experience.'

'I'd be glad to take the chance.'

Aidregh thought a moment. Corlant's expression offered him no hope that she was going to be easily persuaded; she looked gracious, feminine, reasonable, and about as yielding as a female tiger defending a cub. She was magnificent, but she had him in one of the nastiest spots he had ever been in.

'You're not afraid of the Rathemen?' he asked tentatively. 'They may not be as helpful as you postulate.'

'No, I'm not afraid of them,' she said. 'I even think I like Margent, from what little I've heard of him. He seems to be a lot more attractive than Signath, anyhow, or than a lot of other Thrennen men I've met.'

Since this was precisely Aidregh's own opinion, he could not counter it very convincingly, and he did not try. The fact that he felt a surreptitious liking for Margent could not be defended logically, and it did not render Margent or the Rathemen in general one whit less dangerous potentially, but if Corlant was not afraid of them – and it was transparently obvious that she was not, and might never be – then that was that. He brought his last piece of artillery up on to the firing line, absurdly conscious of how small a calibre piece it was, how seemingly ineffectual.

'I still don't see how I can do it,' he said. 'I'm told that the weight allowances on the ships have to be figured to very close tolerances. We can't afford to take anyone with us who doesn't have some absolutely indispensable skill, or isn't otherwise needed in the negotiations. Otherwise we might not arrive. In other words, Corlant, we can't carry any passengers; in one sense or another, we'll all be crewmen.'

'I can be as much of a crewman as Aidresne,' she said. 'His skills only duplicate yours – he's a diplomat, and you'll be handling all the diplomacy. He's going because it's traditional for him to go, and because it's good politics. That makes him a passenger, by your own definition. Isn't that true?'

'Well—' Aidregh stopped and drew a rueful breath. 'Yes, Corlant, it's true. But—'

'What about my father?'

'Oh, now, that's a different case entirely,' Aidregh said with some relief. 'He'll be the flight surgeon; the only one along. He's clearly indispensable.'

'I don't agree,' Corlant said with a sudden and disquieting smile. 'There are surgeons better qualified than he is to make the trip; he isn't even a member of the Aero-Medicine board. He got picked because he's the First Minister's surgeon, and for no other reason. You can't deny it, Aidregh.'

He shrugged helplessly. What she said was so, but was vastly over-simplified; he knew he could not begin to make any impression on her with the thousands of small corollary reasons for these choices. She came forward and took one hand in both of hers, looking up at him with sudden earnestness, like a child.

'Aidregh, please listen,' she said. 'I know it's dangerous. But you're taking Aidresne and my father with you all the same. If you're all killed, where will that leave me? More than half of my life will be destroyed; I'll be nothing. Don't make me face it. It would be much better for me if I died with the rest of you, if that's how it's going to be. You can't condemn me to stay behind, waiting for everyone I love to be destroyed at one blow – and then to keep right on living, just as if an empty life were worth living. It isn't. You know it isn't.'

He knew it well. The ghost of his wife moved briefly in his mind again. What would have been left for him, back in those black hours, if it had not been for Aidresne, the new-born infant to whom she had gladly passed on her own life?

He would not be First Minister of Thrennen now; he would not, probably, be anything but a broken and embittered man, senile and useless in his prime. Only the cherishing forward of that surrendered life had fitted him to take custody of the life of his whole world of Home.

'All right,' he said huskily. 'You can go along, Corlant. I think we need you.'

Her hands tightened on his. He hardly realized that she had kissed him, however lightly, until after she was gone; but the spectral after-impression stayed on his forehead, like the wing-brush of a moth in a spring night, until he had calmed down enough to notice it. In the midst of calamitous doubt, the sensory imprint was like a moment of truth.

Curiously, the press reaction was grudgingly favourable. One widely read, breathless columnist, a great favourite for two decades with the part of the press controlled by the Opposition, dabbed at her eyes and called the arrangement 'divinely handkerchiefy'. Most of the rest of the editorialists were able to keep their noses from running compulsively at the very thought of Corlant's accompanying her father and her lover to Rathe, but they could not find it in their pens to oppose it, either. The best that they could do was to suggest, mostly between the lines, that Aidregh had planned this superb piece of sentimentality from the beginning, to play on the public's heart-strings. Aidregh was content; that line would not get them far, in the face of the fact that the public's heart-strings plainly *had* been struck a resounding twang.

But Aidresne was furious.

'I'm sorry, Aidresne,' Aidregh told him. 'But she *did* ask to go, after all. And this whole reaction to the wedding postponement has given me a handle – an unexpected one, I'll admit – for turning people away from the much more dangerous political implications of the flight. This is one angle Signath *can't* turn his fire on. If he does, he'll just alienate his own followers; everybody thinks the world of you two, regardless of what they think of me. And as long as that's where the major interest lies, I've got to encourage it.'

'But why does everything we do, everything we think or feel, have to be turned into politics?' Aidresne demanded. 'I was already sick enough of having Corlant's every move, and mine, reported on the next day to the whole continent. And now you've got Corlant on what is actually only the second interplanetary flight we've ever attempted – despite the fact that she hasn't any qualifying skills you couldn't find in thousands of other women—'

'She'll make herself useful, I'm sure,' Aidregh said. 'Calm down, Aidresne. The thing is done, and it seems that most of the people approve of it. They may even be right. Suppose we leave her behind, and we all do come to a bad end? Where would she be then? The ex-fiancée of the dead son of a dead First Minister – and without a father to boot?'

'All right, all right,' Aidresne said, almost surlily. 'Please, father, don't be plausible at me. I know your reasons; I still don't like it. I was reconciled to being wired for sound all my married life, but this is something else again. I don't like it, that's all.'

Aidregh had to leave it at that. He was a little afraid that Dr Ni might yet take the same tack – after all, it had been Ni who had first raised this question of sacrificing personal values to political expediency, way back during the eclipse. But Ni seemed to take the whole thing almost as a matter of course. He was much more excited about going on a real spaceflight, a notion which seemed to have shaken him almost entirely out of his world-weariness. Sometimes, indeed, he chattered about it like a breathless adolescent. Told that Corlant would also be making the trip, he merely raised his eyebrows and said abstractedly:

'Oh? Well, if she wants to go . . . I can't say that I blame her— You know, Aidregh, Captain Loris was telling me only this morning that as we approach turnover, we'll have with us a flight of small unmanned radar vessels to scan for missiles while we're unable to scan for them ourselves, and that—'

As for Signath, though his major line of attack had turned out to be somewhat beside the point – evidently he had been as surprised as Aidregh by this reaction from the public – he did not take long to swing into action. The day before the ferry rockets were scheduled to start conveying the expedition to the satellite station, in whose orbit the three ships which would make the actual trip were waiting, Aidregh heard part of one of his speeches. It came in days after it had been delivered, through a recording which had been sent to the office along with the report of the party secretary-general, and went unheard for some days after that; Aidregh had little time for party politicking now. Signath had said:

'Let me remind you all that we have not been told why our First Minister wants to go to Rathe, at the bidding of this creature called Margent. I predict that we will never be told, unless we demand to be told; and I predict that then we will be told lies.

'Let me remind you all that to allow any member of the party in power to negotiate with an enemy is to invite a sellout. Let me remind you all that it was First Minister Aidregh himself who negotiated the previous sellout to Noone. But evidently this was only a very small thing for him.

'It was not enough to betray the whole continent of Thrennen, chiefest of all the nations – until his party began guiding its destinies. No; Aidregh is ambitious. He wants to be the first man in history to sell a whole world. I predict that if this Rathe expedition is allowed, our pro-Rathe First

Minister will come home little better than a lackey of this Margent and his fellow-monsters, unless we prevent it. But we must be firm and resolute; this is not a time for hesitation and soul-searching, but a time for action—'

And so on. It was the expected gambit. Aidregh hoped that at least some of its teeth had been pulled by this really quite irrelevant matter of the wedding postponement.

On the other hand, Aidregh thought with spurious detachment, do gambits have teeth? There I go mixing my metaphors again; Ni says that that's a sure sign that I really don't know what it is that I'm thinking about. Maybe what I really think is that Signath is as dangerous as ever.

But the three ships took off from the satellite station for Rathe on schedule.

VI

And they came down on schedule. As an adventure, the flight was something of a dud.

Aidregh was familiar with that segment of popular fiction which purveyed space flight as something uniquely wonderful in itself, and had always vaguely supposed that it would be. Captain Arpen's tremendous and terrible ordeal on Nesmet had helped to convince him, too. But there was nothing overwhelming about this flight – not for a man so worried over the outcome of the trip, and so loaded with work and responsibility, as to be hardly able to enjoy the present no matter where he was – a man, in short, who was going somewhere because it was important for him to be there, rather than where he had been when he started.

To be sure, the trip was noticeably different from travelling by jet-liner, principally in the large number of additional discomforts involved. Several times during the flight he had meant to take time to look at the stars, and indeed did catch a few glimpses, but they looked just like the stars he had seen from the satellite station: hard cold points, incredibly numerous, unwavering, and giving somehow an impression of iciness, except for the furious vortex of flame which was the Cluster. They were awash in the deepest silence Aidregh had ever known, a silence that even the occasional man-made sound aboard his ship could not dispel, a silence so intense that it had a sound of its own – a soft, distant hissing echo, like surf or the sound in a sea shell. It was the noise of his own blood rushing through the capillaries of his inner ear.

Except for the stars and the flowing silence, he suspected that his first spaceflight was going to turn out to be very like his first air flight: exciting in prospect, uneventful in fact, downright dull in retrospect. That, however, was before turnover, and the subsequent polite invitation from Captain Loris to watch the globe of Rathe from the rear blister as they made their landing approach.

Rathe was no longer a globe at all by the time Aidregh had got himself strapped into his seat. It was already so close that it looked more like a saucer than a sphere – a tremendous expanse of ochre and yellow desert, blindingly bright under its triple illumination, and set here and there with the blue or emerald jewels of lake or oasis. Though he had seen substantially the same view from a telescope at the satellite station four days ago, it was entirely different now, seeing it uncircumscribed by the limits of the telescope's field of view – and growing noticeably larger, minute by silent minute, until it no longer had any edges at all.

'I think I can see the city we spotted in the eclipse photographs,' Aidregh said, squinting. 'Over there, at about twenty degrees, working a third out from the centre of the disc.'

'Yes, that's it,' Loris said, preoccupied. He was not watching through the bubble at all – the heavily leaded, sandwiched layers of plastic and glass were too hard on definition. He had the image of the planet on a large screen, almost in his lap; from time to time the ghostly outlines of instruments were superimposed on the image, as his fingers called them forth from a simple digital keyboard. Occasionally a metre-outline bloomed in red on the screen, as the scanners down below in the unmanned computer section picked up an unusual reading and offered it in the control cabin for inspection; but thus far Loris had done nothing about them but hit the 'kill' bar on his keyboard – the divagations were minor and at random. He seemed to be paying much more attention to the pure musical pipings which filled the air around him: the readings of the four or five instruments which he now most needed to know from minute to minute. Dr Ni had been much intrigued by the discovery that spaceship captains, like Arpen and Loris, had to have perfect pitch.

'Are we landing near there?' Aidregh asked after a moment.

'No, sir,' Loris said. 'We're landing far out in the desert. A five-mile circle, a long way away from any city or oasis. All three ships have to come down inside it.'

The tones in the air made a chord of the inverted 11th. Loris punched a key and the root of the chord nastily; he punched two more. The chord vanished serially, with a mournful 'sfree-sfrong' on the last two notes, and was replaced with the peeping of an oscillator.

'On target,' Loris told his lapel microphone. He added to Aidregh, 'The Rathemen picked the spot.'

'They're not taking any chances,' Aidregh said grimly.

'No, sir. We're being monitored from here on down. If we deviate from our orbit by more than two per cent, we'll never know what hit us.'

Aidregh took the hint and fell silent. A moment later, a blast of organ-thundering, brilliantly white steam blotted Rathe out for several minutes, crushing him back into his seat. The long ordeal of a direct vertical landing was beginning – the ordeal which would exhaust their every drop of reaction mass, and leave them dependent on the Rathemen for enough to get back Home.

And the men of desert Rathe would not be parcelling out any water for reaction mass to potential enemies.

The three ships stood on the desert for perhaps two hours, apparently alone – though Aidregh knew well enough that they were being watched intently from the Cluster before there was any physical sign from the Rathemen. A radio message had acknowledged their announcement of arrival, and then even the radio had become silent; incredibly, there seemed to be no 'regular' programs anywhere on the RF band. Aidregh's party used the time to dog the ships down and make landing parties ready; they were still at the task when the Rathemen finally appeared.

They came racing in from the flat dune-rippled horizon in a horde of low, snaky groundcars, jointed into three sections and running on a multitude of inflated plastic spheres which rolled over the gliding golden sand with no apparent loss of traction. The cars drew up in neat ranks at the feet of the spaceships, and their drivers got out and stood immobile in their robes, each man at the head of his vehicle.

'They don't look like military craft,' Captain Loris said. 'Far too small.'

'No,' Aidregh agreed uneasily. 'But there are a lot of them. It looks like more cars than we have men, at first glance. Didn't they bring any passengers?'

They had brought one: a tall Ratheman who walked unerringly to Aidregh's ship and began to climb the cleats leading to the control cubby. Aidregh hastily sent an escort with a respirator to admit him by the nearest cargo port.

The Ratheman refused the breathing apparatus. He arrived before Aidregh heavily flanked by armed guards, but he did not seem to notice them. In the flesh, he looked much taller than Margent's televised image had suggested the Rathemen were.

'My name is Mareton, servant to Margent,' the Ratheman said in perfect Thrennen. 'We are glad you have come. There is transportation outside for as many of you as will visit with us.'

'Thank you,' Aidregh said formally. 'If you have no objection, we will leave some of our party here.'

'No objection, we will provision them. Those of you who accompany me must leave their weapons behind, however, and be prepared to travel individually. The cars will hold no more than two persons, one of whom must be the driver.'

Aidregh had expected the prohibition of weapons, but this proposed fragmentation of his delegation into units made him uneasy. 'Is there no other form of transportation available?'

'No,' Mareton said. Aidregh thought he saw something very like sleepy amusement in the Ratheman's yellow eyes. He waited for a further explanation, but Mareton evidently had nothing more to say on the subject.

Briefly, Aidregh considered holding out for larger vehicles, but decided against it. He had no proof that larger vehicles even existed, nor would he be in a position to use any such proof even had he had it. Besides, there was probably no danger yet – and he badly wanted to avoid creating a stymie this early in the negotiations.

But it did make him nervous.

On the ground, the little cars proved to be even faster than they had seemed when observed from high up in the nose of the spaceship. Aidregh's car raced over the featureless dunes of the desert with an almost hypnotic gentleness, surging from ridge to trough evenly and without any apparent variation in its smooth flow of silent power. The dunes were not very high; the thin air of Rathe could not produce winds strong enough to produce huge heaps of sand; but since they were the first dunes Aidregh had ever seen, he was impressed. There were no deserts on Home.

The car's chauffeur was as silent as its power plant. He failed to respond by so much as a grunt to Aidregh's essays at conversation in the Rathe tongue, and gave Aidregh nothing to look at but his hunched, burnoosed back. The desert quickly became monotonous; within an hour the three spaceships from Home had disappeared over the horizon, and then there was nothing but sand. Aidregh craned his neck to look out into Rathe's sky for a sight of Home, but he saw nothing but an expanse of almost impossibly deep blue, almost blue-black, in which both the Cluster and the white sun were flaming. Except for the darker colour, it might easily have been the sky of Home; here, as there, it could never be completely night.

Aidregh adjusted his respirator again – the thing kept cutting into his face at one point or another, no matter how he fussed with it – and tried to settle back. Sand, and more sand. Then, at the top of an unusually high dune, perhaps a real hill with a layer of sand over it, he saw the city.

It was only a series of pointed shadows at first, but by the time the car topped the next rise it was markedly closer. For a man accustomed to the low, horizontally-organized architecture of Thrennen it was confusing. The structures were organized vertically, with peaked tops, as though supported by a central mast. Pyramidal caps with sloping sides ending high above the ground in a rectangular or polygonal frame, from which the curtaining walls fell away, also curving, to a wider base among the dunes. Peculiar trees with long trunks and suddenly exploding, frond-clustered crowns grew around their bases, making a green contrast with the panels of colour that soared above them. None of the structures had windows, but some seemed folded in the front; like fabric; others were fronted with canopies supported by poles slanting upwards from among the trees. Here and there a long, diaphanous banner stirred, trailed away along some current in the rare atmosphere, and drooped back again into graceful folds from its high peak. Once, too, Aidregh thought he saw one of the vast folded façades begin to part, as if being thrust to either side at the bottom; but the air was shimmering with heat, and the folds frequently rippled of themselves on that account at this distance – the effect was purely optical. The huge assemblage of pavilions seemed silent and solemn, as though waiting for some event which might never happen at all.

A low domed hill cut off the view, and then the car was wriggling along a valley. There was less sand now; the sides of the valley were rocky. A few minutes later the car was humming towards a low cliff with a cul-de-sac at its end – or, no, not a cul-de-sac, but a dark hole that looked to be little more than a burrow. The car plunged into it without hesitation.

For almost another hour by Aidregh's chronometer, the vehicle continued to race in complete darkness, darting and twisting through one invisible corridor after another. During all this time there was nothing for Aidregh to look at but the soft blue glow of the instruments on the vehicle's dashboard, and the back of his unresponsive driver. By the occasional popping in his ears, he judged that they were going steadily downwards, and after a while he chanced snatching a breath outside his respirator. The air pressure was still low and the humidity was almost non-existent, but it was quite thick enough to breathe without discomfort as long as he was doing nothing but sitting. He took the respirator off with relief.

The car snaked down a dizzy spiral in the darkness and resumed its wriggling, centipede-like run. The air pressure continued to rise, and so did the temperature. The driver made no move. He, like Mareton, had not been wearing any respirator at the start of the journey, and he was not wearing one now; evidently the Rathemen could accommodate a much wider spectrum of pressure and oxygen-tension than the Home people could. It was a point to remember – though doubtless one of the scientists, undergoing a journey very much like this one somewhere else on Rathe, had registered it in far more precise terms by now; had perhaps even evaluated it, which was quite beyond Aidregh's powers.

Dazzling light burst suddenly in upon him, and he flung his arm over his eyes. While he was getting his vision back, the car came to a smooth stop. Blinking, he peered out cautiously.

They had debouched into a small cave, perhaps fifty feet high, brilliantly lit by an overhead glare too bright to see directly. The driver opened the car silently; the moment Aidregh was out, the car scuttled away through a low circular door, like the one which had admitted them. There was one other entrance, cut to admit men rather than vehicles.

For an instant, Aidregh was alone. Then the door opened. Margent came out.

'You made a good journey,' the Ratheman said gravely. 'Come in. There are comfortable quarters inside.'

Numbly, Aidregh allowed the Ratheman to take his arm. He noticed suddenly that he had been holding his breath, and let it out with a long sigh. Had he been expecting, unconsciously, that Margent would . . . would smell bad? He didn't; he had no perceptible odour at all. Aidregh hoped that Margent would be able to say the same of him—Curious that he'd had no such reaction to the driver of the groundcar.

The quarters beyond the door were indeed comfortable, if a little odd by Home standards. The illumination was that same merciless overhead glare, which made everything look bare and cheerless, especially since there was no furniture. Instead, the room was heaped with fabrics of all kinds: blankets, rugs, stuffs like silk. Dr Ni was sitting on one such accumulation, looking remarkably ill at ease. He jumped up with a wordless exclamation as Aidregh came in.

'Hello, Ni,' Aidregh said. 'I'm glad to see you, too. How about the rest of the party?'

'Not here,' Ni said. 'Margent won't tell me where they are.'

'No,' Margent said immediately. 'We have separate quarters for them, that is all. We did not want to put you all in a barracks. This will be your home while you are on our planet.'

'But where are we?' Aidregh said.

'The exact location does not matter. As I think you may have understood, you are many miles inside Rathe; this is one of the shelters we have carved out, in which we hope to save a fraction of our race, should there be war. Your son and Dr Ni's daughter are in another such, with several of your ships' officers, since your custom seems to require that such a couple not be left alone.'

Both Ni and Aidregh grinned at this. The Rathemen's concern for chaperonage would have been grotesque had it not been for the circumstances; but how were the Rathemen to know what customs were not to be violated under any circumstances, and which were merely conventions? Their caution made sense.

Margent did not notice the grins – or chose not to notice

them. 'Others are similarly quartered elsewhere. But this question is of no special moment yet. You will need rest after your trip, and then we may talk about matters of substance.'

'May Dr Ni and I talk to our children, and the other people we brought with us?' Aidregh said.

'No,' Margent said, without expression. 'Not at this time. Nor may you leave these rooms, for the moment. The reasons will be explained after you have rested. I will return tomorrow.'

He went out, with that abruptness with which he had always terminated his interviews. Aidregh and Dr Ni stared at each other.

'You're supposed to call Drash tonight, aren't you?' Dr Ni said.

'Yes.'

'What will happen if you don't?'

Aidregh sat down on the lumpy fabrics.

'I don't know,' he said. 'I'm afraid to think.'

Margent was back the next day, very early, long before Aidregh and Dr Ni had begun to work the stiffness out of their muscles; they had stayed up late in fruitless speculation, and the piled fabrics had not afterwards been kind to their bones.

'There will be food immediately,' Margent said. 'Shall we talk now, Aidregh?'

'By all means,' Aidregh said. 'I don't know what havoc you've already created, Margent, with this imprisonment, but it may not be too late even now. Somehow, in spite of everything, I think you are a reasonable man; I feel it in my bones.'

Margent bowed slightly. 'I do what I can,' he said.

'All right. I have come all this way to accommodate you.

Surely there is something we can do, something decisive, that will make our worlds friends.'

'There may be,' Margent said. 'I did not ask you here for nothing.'

He paused while three silent Rathemen came in with breakfast: a huge circular platter for each of them, bearing dried fruits, a kind of bread, a pot with a long spout out of which a smoky vapour curled and disappeared almost instantly in the dry air. When the servants – guards? – had left, Margent said:

'I must ask you certain questions. For instance: What do you swear by?'

'Nothing, usually,' Aidregh said wonderingly. 'By the Cluster, sometimes. It's not really an oath, only an expletive.'

'I understand. But it means that you have Cluster worship on your planet, or you did at one time? Yes; so do we; we have it still. Now: Do you also have the Three Shadows?'

'Yes, indeed.'

'It could hardly have been otherwise,' Margent said with gloomy satisfaction. 'Now at last I will make myself clear, Aidregh, and then you will understand how enormous a problem faces us both. Cluster worship is very powerful on Rathe, and because we have always been able to see your world from the very earliest times, your planet plays a major role in the religion. We are a custom-ridden people, with ceremonies for everything, all of them governed in turn by the positions of the Three Lights and the Sister World; this very conversation, for instance, cannot be prolonged one minute beyond one hour, for the stars would then be inauspicious. Is this clear, and, more important, is it credible?'

'It is both,' Aidregh said. 'At Home, this system of belief is called astrology; but it is widely discredited and its subscribers are a little shamefaced about it.'

'Not so here,' Margent said. 'There are reasons behind rituals; they establish patterns which facilitate the movement of thought in the desired direction, as music does. When a whole race becomes involved in such customs, it is because that race has goals; when those customs are disrupted, the resentment is likely to be very great. In our case the disruption cannot be tolerated any more. My people absolutely demand that this situation between our worlds be brought to an end. You are not aware of the fact, but our culture has *already* been half destroyed by it. I do not think you can know what a menace you are to us.'

'A menace?' Aidregh laughed shortly. 'I'm aware of it, all right. Most of the weapons involved were built by my order.'

'There you are quite wrong,' Margent said quietly. 'The weapons which menace us are not yours. Those can only kill us, and every man dies in due course. The weapons which have already done such enormous damage are our own.'

'I don't understand.'

'There is a device which we have perfected,' Margent said. 'Our fission bombs are clad in sheaths of a certain metal. When the bombs go off, they will have an effect which will much outlast any immediate destruction they may cause. They will poison your air with a radioactive isotope of this metal, which has a half-life of more than five years. We have enough of these weapons to destroy utterly not only your people, but every form of air-breathing life on your planet, all the way down to the lowliest worm. It is not even necessary for us to hit specific targets. We know that the secret you possess produces vastly greater explosions than our bombs do, for we saw one of the tests; so we know that you can wreck the entire surface of our planet. But we doubt that your bombs will poison our air, except transiently. In deep shelters such as these, some of us may survive.'

Had he been dealing with someone of his own race, Aidregh would have known without question that Margent's face was racked with the deepest of griefs as he said these things, though his voice was quite even. Somehow, Aidregh did not doubt that the emotion was there, nevertheless. He was astonished to find his heart going out to the man; he felt an urgent, irrational impulse to assuage his suffering in some way.

'Still I don't understand,' he said. 'What you tell me is horrifying, of course. But by your own showing, the menace for us is far greater than it is for you.'

'The existence of these weapons is the greatest threat to Rathe that has ever existed,' Margent said. 'They are the reason why your planet is a menace to us – because you have forced us to think in terms of destroying another race. This kind of thinking has been unknown on Rathe for many centuries, and it is ravaging us like a flame. It must be stopped.'

Aidregh and Ni looked at each other, dumbfounded. Aidregh tried desperately to capture some idea of the value system from which Margent's speech must have emerged, but it slipped away from him almost without trace.

'I see where your difficulty lies,' Margent said. 'I will try to explain—'

'Margent.'

'Yes, Aidregh.'

'Are you reading my mind?'

'Yes,' Margent said. 'Do not let it trouble you, it is quite normal. I will explain. Consider, if you can, what our situation has been here on Rathe. As you know, the planet has always been poor in water and in arable land. Furthermore, it is poor in metals, particularly the heavier ones; our present war implements have virtually exhausted the supply. Under these circumstances, we did not develop any extensive physical science. The fact that there have never been any real natural barriers between peoples on Rathe made warfare uncommon even in primitive times, so the major stimulus for physical science was removed, and the lack of supplies for pursuing it inhibited it still further. Thus as we grew older we tended to concentrate on the humanities – the arts, ethics, communication, human behaviour. Under the influence of these studies we eliminated our primitive nations, evolved a common language, reduced our government to next to nothing, eliminated crime, and in general cleared away enough clutter to make it possible for us to attend to serious matters. In the past century we have been exploring the reaches of the mind – not the shadow which bears that name, but the thing itself in the living man. The telepathy which you have noticed is one outcome of these researches, and incidentally a minor outcome.'

'This is an amazing record,' Aidregh said, 'and it's clear proof of what I had suspected all along: that we have a lot to learn from you. But still—'

'I am coming to that point. Think now what happened to us when our first crude radios picked up the broadcasts from your planet – which, because of all that water, was the abode of the soul to our primitive people – and what those broadcasts revealed about you. You were having a war then; it was during the liquidation of the Medani. That crime appalled us all, yet we could do nothing but stand helplessly by while it was committed. And the conviction was slowly borne in upon us that our own time might be coming; that regardless of our own feelings we must prepare some defence against you.

'You will not understand when I say that the ensuing period was like an orgy, but I can compare it to nothing else. For half a century we have hardly had two sane thoughts in succession on Rathe; our minds have been submerged in preparations for blood-letting. We have brought ourselves back to a state of mind where it is possible for us to think of wiping you all out. That event alone has been more devastating for us than any actual war is likely to be. Furthermore it has set back our serious research, we do not know just how far – perhaps by several centuries.'

'How could it do that?' Ni asked practically. 'I can see that it might have halted it for the time being, but surely knowledge already gained can't be unlearned.'

'It can in this field,' Margent said. 'The physical sciences are positively deadly to the highest functions of the mind. The only example I can give you that would be familiar to you is one in ethics: how is it possible to cultivate an ethical sense while you are simultaneously making fission bombs? The two are not only incompatible, they are actively hostile. Similarly I can tell you that a sophisticated science of radio is antithetical to any real command of telepathy. The same antitheses exist throughout the whole range. That is why this hostility between us *must* be ended. The only outcome possible is peace. Your planet and mine are so different that we can find no real grounds for disagreement, let alone disagree so fundamentally as to precipitate a war.'

Aidregh mopped his brow. 'There's no doubt about that,' he said hoarsely. 'But I can't imagine this argument having any force back home. The opposition will laugh it out of existence.'

'Not when they understand it,' Margent said. 'Your people are neophytes in problems of conscience; you do not know what damage has already been done to *you* by these war preparations. But I can tell you what will happen if you should succeed in destroying Rathe without losing a single life on your planet – which I take it would be regarded as the *best* outcome by your opposition.'

'I'm afraid it would.'

'It would be suicide,' Margent said evenly. 'If your race

were to take the blood of ours to itself as a burden, it would never solve its own local conflicts. Your ethical evolution would be stopped in its tracks, and shortly thereafter you would kill each other off.'

There was a long silence, except for a single convulsive swallow from Dr Ni. At last Aidregh said:

'Why couldn't you tell me this before?'

'Because there is more to come that cannot be told in words,' Marent said. 'I have told you that our development did not stop with the humanities; that it has progressed into fields which your race does not even know exist. Out of these researches we propose to give you a weapon, but what could I have said about it over the radio? We have a saying in Rathe: "The colour-blind man may dye his tent red or blue, but he will not dye it in stripes." The best that I could do was to hint at these matters under the general head of "religion", the only word in your language which applies even vaguely to them. They have to be experienced, and that is why we have brought you here. Once you have learned what we mean to teach you, you will find that your argument back home will not lack for force; the future is plain on that point.'

'The *future*!'

'Yes. Fifty years ago anyone of us could have told you accurately and in detail what lies ahead, but what I have called the orgy of war preparations has nearly ruined the faculty. Now it gives us little but vague blurs; but on this question there seems to be no doubt.'

Aidregh was now so used to being stunned that he was beginning to feel that it was his normal state of mind. He said at last, 'Very well, I am in your hands.'

'I am honoured,' Margent said. 'But it is not you, we have discovered, who must undergo this ordeal. Since you have arrived here, we have found that you will be less able to use the experience than others in your party. That is why I have included Dr Ni in this conversation: those we propose to use are Corlant and Aidresne.'

'No!' Ni was on his feet in an instant. 'I won't have it! If anybody—'

'Ni, wait a minute,' Aidregh said, softly but insistently. 'There's no harm intended, can't you sense that? You're still thinking in the Home terms, and they don't apply here. Let's try to understand the thing first.'

Ni looked at him for a moment, and then unclenched his fists slowly.

'If you say so,' he said, shrugging. He sat down again, a listless caricature of Worldly Wisdom, as though his emotional outburst had betrayed him to himself.

'Tell me, Margent, why does it have to be these two and no others?'

'It does not,' Margent said, with what seemed to be obvious reluctance. 'But we think that they alone can undertake the instruction wholeheartedly, and integrate it fully.'

'Because they are young?'

'In part, but only in small part. We were guilty of thinking in inappropriate terms also. It is a fact of nature on Rathe that all men love one another, and we unconsciously expected that the relationship would exist among you too, however imperfectly. But it does not. Of all your party, only four are bound by those ties, and only in Corlant and Aidresne is the tie full and perfect. Since love is the core of understanding, why make anything less serve?'

The point, Aidregh thought, was peculiarly forensic; long training in the less exalted concepts of politics enabled him to detect, through language alone, when an opponent was on the defensive. He looked steadily into the Ratheman's eyes.

'But others among us *could* learn?'

'Perhaps,' Margent said, stiffening slightly. 'We would not

encourage the experiment. Many of our people would be deeply suspicious of it, which would be a poor atmosphere for learning – and the time is very short. Even to Corlant and Aidresne we can teach only certain rudiments, but we hope these will serve the purpose.'

'What do *they* say?' Aidregh asked quietly.

'They have agreed.'

Dr Ni was wringing his hands and looking at the floor; the doctor was obviously in anguish. Aidregh could not help but share his distress, for Margent's wording, even the positions of his body underneath the many robes, telegraphed that his proposals concealed dangers. Aidregh himself would have undergone whatever ordeal Margent had in mind without hesitation, but this proposition was something else again. What, after all, did Margent know about the minds which he was prepared to subject to his wholly mysterious 'education'? What if they broke under the strain? Then war would surely come, and the children would be gone, their sacrifice for nothing— What was it that Ni had said, so long ago? 'You're killing yourself in the name of a set of abstractions.' Himself, yes; but the children?

'I cannot agree out of hand,' he said at last. 'There is at least one stopgap we should try first. You must allow me to call Home, and explain this business of the metal sheaths on your bombs, and ask for patience. I have no technical details to give away, not even the name of the metal involved, and I won't mention the half-life of its isotope. In any event we couldn't revamp our weapons in time, no matter what I inadvertently give away.'

'I was prepared even for that,' Margent said; and now Aidregh was quite willing to be sure that he saw a faint tinge of complacency in the Ratheman's response. 'It will not work, Aidregh; it is a method of fear. Nothing will serve now but methods from love.' The glowing eyes were regarding him steadily. Was Margent actually *pitying* him? 'But you may try it. There is radio equipment ready for you in the next room.'

Aidregh almost ran out of the chamber. Thus far, Margent had not read what was going on at the deeper levels of his mind – either his success at reading its surface thoughts and anticipating them, or the planet-wide impairment of such psychic functions which he had described, was impeding any real penetration in depth. Aidregh's escape left Dr Ni staring alternately at the Ratheman and at the floor.

When Aidregh came back, his face was ghastly and he knew it, but there was nothing he could do about it. His shoulders felt as though they were being dragged down by the clinging hands of a billion dying people. Dr Ni sprang to his feet with a choked curse. Margent did not move, but the fires that burned in his hooded eyes leaped and flickered.

'Too late,' Aidregh said hollowly. 'You were right, Margent. There is already a coalition government there. Signath worked faster than I'd dreamed he could. The overnight silence helped him. I told him what you had told me, but I'm the last person in the world – in two worlds – that he would listen to. He gives you three days to release us all. After that, after that—' His voice failed him completely.
Dr Ni staring alternately at the Ratheman and at the floor.
shouted. 'Deadlines in total war! Announcing the date of an attack—'

Margent raised his slender hand. Ni choked off his fury with obvious reluctance.

'It cannot matter,' Margent said gently. 'We would never fire first in any event. We will see your shots coming, in plenty of time to launch our own weapons before yours get here; and so we will both be destroyed. We will respect the deadline; why not?'

'As you say, it makes no difference,' Aidregh said huskily,

'The war has begun. We have all lost; the end is upon us.'

'No,' Margent said. 'Not quite. Give your consent, and it can all be changed.'

VII

For the rest of the day, Aidregh moved about the room in a dull, aching fog, picking at the food that was brought in, exchanging no more than a monosyllable or two with Dr Ni. When, after an eternity, the light dimmed for the night, he found that despite his exhaustion it was impossible to sleep. At last he heaved himself up on one elbow.

'Ni?'

'Urhm?'

'Ni. Listen to me. He's wrong.'

'Who's wrong? Margent? Of course he's wrong. He's a madman.'

'No, he isn't mad,' Aidregh said. 'He's a wise man. We've been underestimating him, and all the Rathemen. His proposition is logical: if there's no way out of this except through the children, then we have to give them the chance. After all, they *have* consented.'

Dr Ni sighed and sat up. 'I thought it would come to this in the end,' he said, his voice charged with bitterness. 'But not for me, Aidregh. Politics stops here for me, no matter how much farther you're prepared to go. As far as I'm concerned, both worlds can die, if this has to be the price for saving them – either of them.'

'But what price are you talking about, Ni? We don't know what's planned, and Margent can't describe it to us. We haven't the terms. There's a whole new science here, a whole new way of thinking that doesn't even exist as far as our language is concerned. All he can say is that he can give us a weapon that will stop the war. How do we know it mightn't also be a great gift? What is it that we're protecting the children from, anyhow? It might well be something marvellous.'

'Yes. Or something deadly.'

'Something so deadly that we have to save them from it – to die under our own bombs? Is *that* mercy, Ni?'

'It may well be,' Dr Ni said, his voice harsh and flat. 'I can't quite tell whose side you're on. But there's one thing I know as a doctor: that of all the things in the universe that a child needs to be protected from, his parents are usually the first. You're beginning to sound like a classical example of that law.'

'I know it,' Aidregh said. 'I don't mean for an instant to let the children go through with this, any more than you do. Politics stops there for me, too; you taught me that. I was only trying to show that Margent is not a madman. He's wrong, but that doesn't automatically make a man crazy.'

Dr Ni sighed again.

'I suppose not,' he said. 'You confuse me, Aidregh. Please tell me very simply and straightforwardly what the Isle you're talking about.'

'I mean to take this training myself.'

Ni was silent a long time. At last he said slowly, 'Margent won't like it.'

'No, he won't. He's said pretty plainly that I'm not the right person for the job, and furthermore I think his reasons are probably pretty good. But he's unable to pretend that *only* Corlant and Aidresne have any chance of success. He says only that for anybody else to take the job would make it very hard. All right. I'm used to doing things the hard way. After a pretty long life I'm convinced that there is no other way.

'That's a dogma,' Ni said. 'Why shouldn't I take it on, instead of you? Corlant's my daughter. And at least I've had some scientific training; I might make a better subject than you would.'

'I doubt that. I think scientific training is the *last* prerequisite for whatever Margent has in mind. The science involved is obviously nothing like anything we know. And the decision is mine, Ni. I will not allow Aidresne's life, or the life of Home, to hang from the capacities of any man but myself. I am not going to step down now and let the children carry the burden, or let you do it, either. That burden is mine, and no one else's.'

'But how do you know it will do any good at all?' Ni demanded. 'Margent's a mystic. How can you believe anything he says? Half of it sounds insane.'

'Signath isn't a mystic. Is *he* sane?'

Dr Ni released a third long, ragged sigh, apparently without being aware of it. 'I'm not even sure that *I'm* sane by now,' he said. 'Corlant is my daughter, that's what I keep coming back to. I'm trying to be reasonable, but I have to think of her first. If Margent thinks she's the most competent—'

'Do you think that you're alone in this room, Ni?' Aidregh said bitterly. 'Aidresne has been my whole life since my wife died, and Corlant is the only meaning that his world has. How can I think less of her than I do of him, if that's how he feels? But there's no chance that we can all just lie back and wait for somebody else to take on this job. Either I let Corlant and Aidresne do it, or I take it on myself, as I came here to do. That's what I'm going to do.'

'You won't let me tackle it?'

'No. You would fail.'

There was a muffled choking sound in the dimness. Aidregh felt as though he had already become a moral monster; the man was, after all, his friend. Then, huskily, Dr Ni said:

'I think I would. So might you.' A long pause, filled with irregularly drawn breaths. 'The Cluster help us all if you do, Aidregh – but you have my consent. Is that what you wanted?'

'Yes,' Aidregh said. 'As you say, Corlant is your daughter. I can't refuse to let her do what she's volunteered to do. That was up to you.'

Dr Ni lay down with his back to Aidregh. If he knew that Aidregh had led him a full 270° away from his original stand, he gave no sign of it; nevertheless, Aidregh sensed that a friendship was ending, here in the darkness. He did not attempt to speak to Ni again that night.

After a while, he too was asleep, but it was a sleep filled with portents and without rest – an underground sleep, which would never see the roses of the day. After a while, it became tenanted with a vision: Aidresne's dead mother. She did not speak either, but her eyes were glistening with sorrow and incredulous reproach.

Margent did not like it. He arrived early the next morning with his two guards, and Mareton; they made small talk through breakfast, and when the guards left, Margent said, 'We must have your decision now, Aidregh.'

His face was stony. Evidently he had already gathered through his mind-reading the essence, if not the details, of Aidregh's decision. Nevertheless Aidregh took pains to spell it out with painful clarity. Throughout the recital neither of the Rathemen's faces moved a muscle.

'This makes everything very difficult,' Margent said after a short silence. 'Most of us on Rathe are deeply suspicious of this project in any event, and do not view the reaching of the *voisk* forces to any of you with approval. It is perhaps analogous to the giving away of military information on your planet. Only the endorsement of the Margents made it possible to make the offer at all.'

'The Margents?' Ni said. 'There's more than one of you?'

'There are twelve,' Margent said, with a preoccupied gesture. 'The name goes with the office. Each of us has full and constant access to the memories of all the others now alive, and all of those who preceded us in the office. Thus we are all the same person, even second by second. The accumulation of memories is more than powerful enough to make us look alike, as well, though we are not genetically related. Our appearance is that of the first Margent, who was the first to realize that memory depends totally on trans-temporal mind contact – and live through the discovery long enough to make use of it.'

For some reason, this did not make Aidregh feel any more sanguine. It was, after all, the *voisk* force, or one of several, that he had apparently volunteered to expose himself to. He said, 'I'm sorry that the decision will make it more difficult; but it is the only decision I could have made.'

'Very well,' Margent said stiffly. 'You will be very closely watched, Aidregh, by observers largely hostile to you. At the first sign of faltering of your purpose, or of failure to use the instrument properly, the experiment will be at an end. It would not have been so for Corlant and Aidresne, but since you are chief of state of your planet, caution can dictate no less.'

'Precisely how would the experiment "end"?' Aidregh asked steadily.

'Why, by ending it, and holding you all hostage to your planet's good behaviour,' Margent said. 'Of course if you are far advanced in manipulating the *voisk* force before any wavering becomes evident, you will be proportionately more dangerous and may be cut down where you stand. But in view of the ultimatum under which we labour, I can hardly see what practical difference that makes.'

'No, of course not.'

'Do you want to proceed under those conditions?'

'Yes,' Aidregh said.

'Very well. We have three days. I think we will get very little sleep.'

VIII

They took Aidregh to the surface, through a complex network of stony corridors which he found impossible to memorize. He found himself at last inside one of those huge, many-coloured tents which he had seen during his trip across the desert. Its peak was shrouded in dimness. Light fell towards the floor – which was smooth-raked sand, for the pavilion was a true tent without foundations, for all of its size – from a sort of censer which hung half-way down.

Ten of the twelve Margents were there, which Aidregh found upsetting in itself. They looked, as Margent had warned him, exactly alike, and sounded exactly alike. Although their robes differed in small details, Aidregh had lost track of which one was 'his' Margent within a few minutes. Perhaps there had never been such a person as 'his' Margent; they might easily have spelled each other before the television cameras without his being aware of it. To clear this irrelevant confusion out of his path, he quickly adopted the stratagem of regarding the one that was speaking as 'his'. It worked poorly, but it was better than no stratagem at all.

'What we are going to teach you, we hope, is a trick,' Margent told him, sitting down on a carpet among the others. 'Obviously it would be impossible to teach you a whole science in three days – or even enough of it to let you enter the field as an investigator on the lowest level. But if we can give you enough understanding to enable you to perform one trick, that should serve the purpose.'

'Not a very flattering assessment,' Aidregh said grimly.

'But a true one. Who was your greatest genius in physics a dozen dozen years ago?'

'A man named Arod,' Aidregh said, puzzled. 'He discovered the electromagnetic spectrum and worked it out mathematically. I don't know the details.'

'The fact is sufficient; that was an impressive achievement. Now, suppose you could bring this man Arod forward into the present era. Could you teach him nuclear physics in three days?'

'Hm-m-m,' Aidregh said. 'No, we couldn't. He'd be able to learn just enough to realize that such a field of knowledge existed. He'd be able to perform a few tricks with apparatus we had set up for him, and he'd go back to his time with a splitting headache.'

One Margent smiled briefly. 'After he had returned to his own time, could he then refine the power metals, compute neutron capture cross-sections, and set up his own reactor?'

'No. He'd probably just die of frustration. Believe me, Margent, I'm convinced. I'm no Arod; learning one trick is good enough for me. What is the trick?'

All of the Margents frowned simultaneously and looked at each other. For the first time, their expressions reflected real uneasiness, or at least uncertainty.

'We are going to have to answer that by talking around it,' one of them said at length. 'Your language simply does not contain the necessary terms, and to substitute into it the appropriate terms from our language would just result in meaningless noise for you. We are going to teach you to manipulate an energy, one of what we have called the *voisk* forces, which can assist you to sway an audience.'

Aidregh was about to exclaim 'Is *that* all?' when he saw all the Margents, and Mareton too, leaning forward tensely. The movement was so slight inside their concealing robes that he had almost missed seeing it entirely.

He drew a deep breath and said instead: 'Very well. Go on.'

The Margents and Mareton leaned back again, and some of the tension went out of the cathedral-like atmosphere of the huge tent. Evidently, Aidregh thought, one of the rules of conduct – or of the science itself, perhaps – made failure to take the right attitude less heinous if it was unvoiced, or thought better of. A cross-relation between the words-v.-works doctrine of ethics, and the observer-effect of physics? In any event, it had been a near thing; he would have to keep the rule constantly in mind.

'There are several words in your language which skirt what we have in mind,' a Margent said. 'One of them is *empathy*; another is *charisma*. Neither one is the power we are talking about. Such words as sympathy, warmth, accessibility, appeal, personality – they all fall into the same area. None of them describes the power, either, however.'

Aidregh began to see another reason why the road before him was going to be stony. He tried to imagine a concept-area bracketed or bounded by all these negative definitions, but instead they all overlapped in his mind and left no room for a hole through which some unnamed concept might peer.

'Can you show it in operation?' he said. 'A functional definition should be possible – one which doesn't depend on semantic content.'

'Certainly; that is the next step. Mareton, will you read to us?'

From his robes, Mareton drew forth a small scroll, unrolled it, and began to read in a dry, precise voice:

'"In the epoch 480, while the policy of proportional water doles was still in effect despite its inequities, the use of ground water for industrial purposes rose by twelve gross megabires per cycle, while additional supplies to the sum of a gross megabires was drawn from standing sources – such as lakes and oases. Recovery from rainfall during the same period fell a gross megabires as standing sources lost surface area, forcing the transfer of the major part of the load to the pipeline system, which was by then grossly inadequate to carry it. Nevertheless, the proportional dole system was maintained for another epoch of cycles, thus completing the breakup of the nation-tribes upon whom the principal shortages fell. It now appears that this political effect was what had been intended all along by the devisers of the dole system."'

Aidregh swallowed. Though the story was from the history of another planet, he had never heard anything that had struck the note of tragedy more deeply, or in such sure prose; his throat felt positively dry. Only its apparent irrelevancy to the *voisk* forces made him hesitate to say so – yet he was perfectly convinced that, had he been born an artist, he might have made an immortal epic out of Mareton's precis.

The Margents were all watching him silently. Slowly, he recovered his detachment, and thought back over what Mareton had read, as carefully as a man walking on new-frozen ice. Tragedy? No. *In esse*, perhaps, but not *in posse*. What Mareton had read him had been a piece of unfeeling statistics. And he had very nearly wept over it!

'I see,' he said at last. 'It's a striking trick, and I can see where it would be valuable in politics. Does it work with a large crowd? Or does it thin out?'

'It works over interplanetary distances with no detectable diminution, like all the *voisk* forces; we tested that during our Nesmet expedition, of which you know. The only physical requirement is that the audience be able to see *or visualize* the speaker. The audience may see a televised image, a still photograph, a painting, a caricature, or simply a memory, so long as it has some eidolon of the speaker in the visual circuits of the brain.'

Even Aidregh's small knowledge of physics told him that this was quite implausible – indeed, irrational. Since he had never been trained as a scientist, however, he found himself able to get over that mental hurdle with comparative indifference. He wondered whether Ni would have been able to clear it.

'Did you use this to bring me to Rathe?' he said suddenly.

'In part,' Margent admitted composedly. 'But you were not compelled; this force cannot be used to convince the subject of an unreal situation. The logic of events must always be in tune with it, as it was in your case. Now we will ask you to try it, Aidregh.'

'But I still don't know how—'

'We were aware of that. Try it anyhow.'

Mareton rose and handed him the scroll. The object was clumsy for a man used to books, but after a moment Aidregh discovered how to handle it: the two rolls could be spread between the hands so that the desired paragraph was held taut before his eyes. What little of the rest of the text he could see was as dull as the paragraph Mareton had read – and that was appallingly dull, now that he himself had to make it sound convincing. But he did the best he could, terribly conscious of the intent regard of the Rathemen.

'A total failure,' Margent said gravely when he had

finished. As his heart sank sickeningly within him, another Margent added, 'Do not be alarmed. Another negative demonstration was what we were aiming at. You needed to know what this *voisk* force was *not*, on the operational level. You have just summed that up.'

'How did I do that?' Aidregh demanded incredulously.

'By using nearly every technique your world has evolved for getting along *without* the force. You read the paragraph with great eloquence. Your tone laid heavy emphasis upon the little bit of human content the passage has. Your bodily expression – the communication method your culture calls "parataxis" – reinforced your every point. Your diction was clear, controlled, elegant, yet it filled the whole pavilion without the slightest sense of strain. The variations, in volume, in huskiness and other pitches suggesting emotion, were as precise as music. In other words, you made as much of the passage as a truly great actor or politician could make of it.

'And not one bit of this is pertinent or useful to you now. Not one bit of it has anything to do with the trick *we* want to teach you.'

For a moment, Aidregh sat stunned. Yet it was true: while Mareton had been reading that same passage, he had employed not one of the highly developed techniques of speaking to an audience which Aidregh used as a matter of course. He had simply read it – even droned over it. Yet the emotional impact had been profound.

There was really nothing in the passage that *deserved* the elaborate art of rhetoric, though that art could heighten it spuriously. For this audience, such heightening was obviously worse than useless – it was actually in the way of whatever they were trying to make him understand.

And by the way they were looking at him now, he realized that he had already reached the first test. He was to get no more help past this first stage in his understanding. If he failed to integrate and use all the negative definitions which he now had, in profusion, the experiment would be over.

And he would fail both the children and the world of Home.

'May I try it again?' he said at last.

'Yes,' a Margent said, without expression. 'Once more.'

He read the passage through to himself. What had he actually felt, *in himself*, while Mareton had been gnawing aloud this dry bone of economic history? He forced himself to go slowly, trying to recall each emotion as it had surfaced, almost word by word, holding each new memory in the forefront of his mind, in the hope of piling up that cumulative feeling of total consent which Mareton had provoked in him.

It was horribly difficult. For the first time, he had a dim appreciation of what it might be like to compose an opera.

Then, slowly, he began to read aloud. His voice sounded lifeless in his ears, but he tried to pay no attention to that. Instead, he 'scored' the text like a composer, inside his own head, with the memories of how it had made him feel when Mareton had read it to him.

By the time he reached the last word, he was trembling, and drenched with sweat despite the almost total dryness of the air in the tent. Nothing he had tried to do in all his life before had been so difficult as this.

The Margents and Mareton listened gravely, their yellow eyes watching him with a hooded intentness. Afterwards, the hazy reaches of the pavilion were quiet for what seemed to be hours.

'Weak,' one of the Margents said at last. 'And considerably garbled. But there was some transmission. You have felt your way to the beginning; you have the concept at least intuitively.'

Mareton nodded. 'He has it,' he agreed. 'But now he must attempt the real problem: making it work.'

Dr Ni was still awake when Aidregh, after eighteen gruelling hours, was returned to the underground apartment for a few hours' rest. Though Aidregh's nerves screamed for sleep, he saw at once that the suspense had already driven the doctor nearly into hysteria. There was nothing for it but to describe, as briefly as possible, what had happened to him on the surface.

'This is all so subjective,' Ni said, gnawing at what was left of a fingernail. 'Nothing that can be measured – just a set of feelings, that get reflected in someone else's feelings. Somehow I can't see how you can trust it. Especially not with so many lives hanging from it—'

'Oh, it can be measured,' Aidregh said wearily. 'The test in the tent was only the beginning. Then they took me outside, through the city, to another pavilion – a squat, octagonal affair much bigger in volume than the first one. It was a laboratory of some kind, obviously. Machines on benches, scattered all over the floor. Most of them looked to me as if they'd been put together by a skilled ignoramus trying to pass as a genius: breadboard affairs, half wire, a quarter plumbing, a quarter collage and garbage.

'But I didn't say so; I'd learned that much, at least. Margent – one of him – told me that all the apparatus operated on one part or another of the *voisk* spectrum, and demonstrated several of them. For instance, there was a device that seemed to be a sort of *voisk* transducer; of them all, it looked to be the closest to pieces of electronic apparatus I've seen on Home. He had Mareton do the trick they're trying to teach me, and showed me the tracings it produced. Then he ran off comparison-curves from other parts of the spectrum, like the precognitive and the mind-reading areas he described before. There's no doubt but that the *voisk* forces can be measured, once you've enough of a grip on them to feed them through appropriate instruments.'

He paused a moment, realizing just how what he was about to say was going to sound to Ni. But he was too weary to tackle the extra job of copy-reading his memory; it was all he could do to tell the story unedited.

'The question is,' he said, 'just what constitutes an appropriate instrument. After Margent had run the various curves, he pointed out to me that the electron tubes in the transducer had been dead all along. There wasn't even any power source provided for them; the only power the instrument was using was going directly to the image-orthicon. To prove it, he pulled all the tubes out of the chassis. The thing still functioned.'

'That can't be,' Ni said, sitting up abruptly.

'I can testify that it can be; it happened. And that isn't all. The next thing he did was to slide the chassis out of the apparatus entire, and substitute a wiring diagram, attached to the orthicon leads with clips.'

'And it still worked?' Ni demanded.

'It worked beautifully.'

'Then it's nothing but a conjurer's cabinet,' Ni said harshly. 'I'm sorry, Aidregh, but they're making game of you. The whole thing is a hoax; it can't be anything else.'

'A hoax for what purpose?' Aidregh said. 'Margent knows that we're all under a sentence of death, dated day after tomorrow. Why would he be killing time playing parlour games to fool me?'

'He's trying to frighten you into accepting his terms—'

'Nonsense; I've already accepted them. All he asked us to do was to undertake this training. Besides, Ni, that wasn't the only such demonstration that I saw. All the machines in that tent were analytical devices of one kind or another. There was one that behaved rather like a spectograph. Margent put a piece of live lung tissue into it, and it gave him back an analysis, by weight, of every chemical element in the sample, including the gases trapped in the alveoli. Then Mareton shook up a stack of five gross of cards, each one of which was marked with the *symbol* of one of twelve chemical elements, and gave the machine a random fifty of the cards to scan – *inside a lead tank.* The machine analysed the distribution of the symbols just as promptly, paying no attention to what elements went to make up the paper of the cards, or the lead in the tank walls. It will also give a chemical analysis of an object working from a photograph; I saw it do that, too.'

'And then,' Dr Ni said with deep disgust, 'Margent busted all its tubes, cut all its connections, and immersed it in thick, electrolytic glue – and still it functioned. Eh?'

'Not at all,' Aidregh said, trying to conceal his sudden, exhausted irritation. 'You can't cut the connections on such a device, no matter what they're made of. That was part of the demonstration. Devices that handle any *voisk* force don't need any power from the electromagnetic spectrum, but they do depend utterly upon connectivity. The laws they obey don't follow the quantitative rules of physics; instead, they're wholly topological. You can rob such a device of its power-pack, or of miles and miles of copper wire, or of whole sets of components, and they'll still work. But you must supply some token connection to take the place of the connection you've broken. If the device is operating from a wiring diagram, and you erase one schematic lead, one line on the paper – floomp! The thing goes dead.'

'Ah,' Dr Ni said, no less dubiously than before, but with less tension in his voice. 'Well, that makes a little sense now – a very little. It's still pretty mystical, Aidregh. But then, I . . . I never did understand topology very well, I must confess.'

'I'd barely even heard of it until today,' Aidregh said. He was forced to stop suddenly and stifle a yawn. Exhaustion was pouring over his brain like a torrent of smooth ink; he would be obliterated utterly in a moment. 'But it seems to be vital here. And there's this: what counts is the topological manifold *in the mind*, not in the machine. The machines are just crutches, for me, because I need crutches; the time left is too short for me to learn how to do without them. But sooner or later, they have to be discarded; sooner or later, like any crutch they only get in the way.'

This time the yawn caught him unawares. He fell back among the cushions, the whole world hurtling whirligig in whistling hurrahs around his humming head.

'Ni . . . excuse me . . . good night—'

In scarcely another second he was asleep, in a black nightmare in which children cried and would not stop; and then, light was spilling into his eyes again, and someone was shaking him gently. It was Mareton.

'Wake up, Aidregh,' the Ratheman said stolidly. 'This is our last day.'

IX

The first half of the day was a blur. Though Aidregh's nerves were on a hair-trigger from lack of sleep, his memory for small incidents seemed to be almost drugged, so that within five minutes after some new project had begun, he could hardly recall what the last one had been.

And there were all kinds of emotional undercurrents which he could apprehend without identifying. He was seeing other Rathemen beside the Margents and Mareton now, and most of them did not bother to conceal their hostility. He was convinced that few of them would have spoken to him at all, were it not for the overwhelming authority of the Margents.

But the training proceeded, now on a level where the experiments and tests made almost no sense to him. Evidently they had wanted his conscious understanding only of those points which had been demonstrated to him yesterday. Now, instead, they were drilling him, reaching him by rote, and did not care whether he understood the material he was learning or not. Nor was it his memory they were drilling, but some other part of his mind, of the very existence of which he was unaware; he knew only that he did not know.

Many of the exercises, however, plainly required the use of some kind of judgment or discrimination, although from what basics he again could not say. He was shown a tightly rolled scroll and asked to throw out an emotional reaction to the argument written on it, regardless of the fact that he did not even know what the subject matter was. He was shown a photograph, on glass, of some nearly transparent and quite shapeless object, and told to give it two names – a familiar and a formal one. He was given a set of tones to listen to, and asked to select out sequences which might apply to himself, to Dr Ni, to the children, to Margent. And above all, he was shown Rathemen, scores of them, and was told to talk to them, subject matter unimportant, while the Margents and Mareton closed their eyes and listened as though his every banal word might conceal some universal truth. Sometimes the outcome – always undetectable to Aidregh – seemed to please them. More often, it did not. But gradually, the incidence of successes or partial successes seemed to be increasing.

This would have encouraged Aidregh, had he had some idea of what he was succeeding at.

In the end he was forced to form his own analogy, since the Rathemen would offer no explanation at all. It seemed to him that what he was being trained in was something akin to spot diagnosis – that art of the born physician who looks at the patient and *knows* what the man is suffering from, eliciting the physical signs of the disease to be thorough, but invariably getting confirmation from them of his first three-second guess. The analogy disturbed him, since it again raised the question of his wisdom in refusing to let Dr Ni take his place.

Still, Ni had no special reputation as a diagnostician; perhaps he was too much of a sceptic. Besides, there was no way of knowing whether or not the analogy was correct.

'Enough,' Margent said sharply. 'The last six responses have been sterile repeats. There is simply no point in going any farther.'

Aidregh looked up at the Ratheman, his heart freezing solid.

'So soon?' he whispered.

'I am afraid so. I am a little surprised myself. But we have exhausted every training device we can bring to bear in so short a period; the pattern now is fixed.'

'Hopelessly?'

'Nothing is hopeless,' Margent said. 'But the rest must be up to you.'

'I don't understand.'

'You have the trick in some measure now,' Margent said. 'You know what it is, and you can use it consciously – that is, at will. What this means is that you now have a crude but effective technique – and technique is all that anybody can be taught. How well you use the technique, and how powerful it is in your hands, is entirely personal. We cannot teach you that. All scientists know scientific method, but only a few make great discoveries; all musicians can read music, but not all write great music. It is like that.'

'I see.' It was not as bad as he had supposed when Margent had called the halt a few moments ago, but it was bad enough. 'But Margent, if those analogies are sound, you must have some estimate of my talent. Teachers always develop such an estimate. What is it?'

Margent looked at him gravely. Such estimates are more often wrong than right, as I see you know.'

'That's perfectly expectable. Nevertheless, I want to hear yours.'

Margent seemed to commune briefly with his alter egos, and then spoke decisively. 'As matters stand now, you should be able to sway a small group, particularly if that group is made up of persons who do not know what it is that you are doing – as would of course be the situation anywhere on your planet. But the impulse is weak at the source. To carry absolute conviction, it will have to develop much greater force, and there we cannot help you at all, or tell you how to do it. Either you have the resources or you do not. We cannot know.'

Aidregh thought a moment. 'How about machine amplification?'

'Perfectly possible,' Margent admitted. 'But of no value. It does not improve a bad piper to make his pipe sound four times as loud. You must improve the man – which cannot be done by machine. It cannot be "done" at all; the man himself must do it, no one else.'

Abruptly, there seemed to be some sort of argument, almost a quarrel, going on among the Rathemen. Mareton said, 'Test?' and two or three Margents spoke at once, then Mareton and several more Margents, then the first Margent again – all in single cryptic explosions of words, all the more difficult to follow because they were spoken in the Rathe tongue.

Destructive. Crucial time. Conditions. Tension, Cluster. Favourable. Not so. Mass opposition. Critical factors. (Unknown word.) Present it? Just. Affirm. Affirm. Affirm. Affirm— Agreed.

'We think,' Margent said, 'that you should be asked if you will give a concert.'

'A – concert?' Aidregh said, goggling.

'Yes. The word is a poor one for what we have in mind, but it is the closest we can come in your language. It is meant to convey that the only way to assess talent is to show it before an audience. Tomorrow, if you are willing, we can give your gift the most critical examination it is ever likely to be asked to sustain. The circumstances in the stars are peculiarly right for it, as my colleagues remind me. Would you consent?'

'You want me to ... to give a speech? Before a Rathe audience?'

'Exactly. If you can sway them, you can carry your own world by acclamation. Especially with the stars situated as they are now.'

The idea was breath-taking, and more than a little terrifying. Somehow, too, the references to the stars were almost as unsettling as the proposal itself. Nothing that he had experienced on Rathe had increased his confidence in astrology one iota; Margent's implicit endorsement deepened the air of unreality which had always been the chief obstacle to his learning anything at all from the Rathemen.

'It will be dangerous,' Margent added. 'The hostility will be considerable. Many, perhaps a majority, will be waiting to see you fail. And if you do, you will almost surely have to be helped down from the podium.'

'Why?'

'Because of the reaction. It would probably leave you something less than an idiot.'

'If I fail, I'll welcome losing my mind,' Aidregh said, with bitter conviction. 'And what if I succeed?'

'There the reaction might be important to you. Possibly it would advance your power and control by some years;

confidence is important in these matters. But it will not be easy.'

'I'm sure it won't,' Aidregh said grimly. 'But I'll try it. Of course.'

The amphitheatre on the far side of Rathe was so vast that it had even shown on the photographs Captain Arpen had taken; the Home assessment team had taken it to be an ancient meteor crater. The heaped terraces, which now were filling with robed Rathemen, seemed like the engineering transformation of immense talusslopes. Looking upward from the centre of the bowl, Aidregh tried to estimate the number of Rathemen who were already occupying those stony benches, and failed. The total was easily above half a million, but how much above it he could not begin to guess. The floor of the crater alone might have held a small town. The dyed robes moved like dots in a colour-television transmission, each one clearly picked out by the light of the Cluster, which was rising over the eastern wall.

'It has been many years since we last attempted anything even resembling this,' Margent was saying. 'The omens for it are good, but I misdoubt the reading a little. So much of it is without precedent, and we have lost so much in fifty years of regression.'

Aidregh said nothing; he was almost totally preoccupied with what he was going to say. On a bench six tiers up he could see Aidresne, Corlant, and Dr Ni; he had been unable to exchange more than a few words with them, but he had tried to be reassuring. As a first test of his trick, it had not been successful; their foreheads showed furrowed and wan above their respirators. If there was anyone else from the home expedition here, he could not spot them.

The movement along the great stone steps had almost ceased now. The amphitheatre was full. The Cluster continued to rise, occupying half of what sky could be seen from inside the amphitheatre's walls, and filling the rest with glare. It was like being at the bottom of a hot, shallow tropical sea, whose waters were rippleless, shadowless white light. The thin air was motionless.

'We are ready to begin,' Margent said.

After a moment's hesitation, Aidregh stepped on to the pure white slab which was to be his podium. Though the acoustics of the amphitheatre would have made his voice reach to the topmost benches, he could not speak in the air of Rathe; he had a tiny microphone inside his respirator. The respirator would also mask any expression, however impassioned, his face might wear.

The thousands upon thousands of Rathemen looked down upon him, motionless, unspeaking; the great bowl was utterly silent. At Aidregh's side, Margent seemed to be carved from stone. The sky was full of flame.

'I expect to succeed,' Aidregh told them. 'I expect this because you can do no more for me than what you have done. You are not gods, and you have not proposed to solve all our problems for us.

'Whether or not I succeed depends upon me, not upon you. It depends upon my alertness, my devotion, my purity of intention. There could still be war between us – perhaps not immediately, but in a few generations. You cannot make it impossible for me to choose anything but peace, for that would be as ruinous for you as war tomorrow would be. You must leave me the conscious choice, because these decisions are evolutionary turning-points for you, as well as for us.

'If we – Rathemen and Homemen – survive this crisis, I am perfectly prepared to devote the rest of my life to making another one impossible. Nothing less will serve. But we have already served one another well, and we will continue to need each other in the years to come – as long as the question of the Third Race, is unsolved.

'By this I mean the race that landed on the planet we call Nesmet, before either we or you did. Do you know more than we do about them, which is nothing? I think not. But their camp was plainly an observation station, just like yours and ours. Who could they have been looking at but us – both of us? And why?

'We may have to be glad – *both of us* – that we each built weapon emplacements facing outward from each other. We may have to shoot in that direction some day. I know that your faith in that kind of defence is very limited; but suppose we were to combine our very different approaches to the real universe – whatever that may be – and develop them in co-operation? I think we are fortunately situated for it, though we have our hands on each other's throats for the moment. Our researches in physics are not likely to interfere with your studies in the *voisk* spectrum if we do not force them upon you, as we have done up to now. But you may well find applications of our findings that you might never be able to discover for yourselves. The obverse holds true for us.

'Any Third Race that approaches our system with unfriendly intention thereafter may find such an approach highly unwise.'

He paused, though he did not want to; breathing inside the respirator was difficult after a prolonged speech. As he struggled to calm his chest, he became aware that something was happening. He could not tell what it was. Nothing had changed, and yet there was a sense of enormous purport in the air around him, as though invisible agencies and powers were moving through it upon some unguessable business. The Cluster was now directly overhead, a supernal mass of star-fire shutting out the whole of the sky. The feeling in the air was something like a wave of mass emotion, such as he had felt once or twice from mobs; yet at the same time it was like moving ungrounded through a powerful electrostatic field, with the hair standing up, nimbuses crackling on the fingertips, the sense of being within a step or a spark of death – and yet, nothing was moving, nothing but shadows.

Shadows! With a sharp hiss of indrawn breath, Aidregh looked up. It was true.

His own world of Home was eclipsing the Cluster. The vortex of star-fire was already eaten away by almost a third.

So this was what Margent had meant by saying that the stars were favourable! There was already a chill in the air, not just an affect, but a real drop in the temperature. Rathe was throwing its heat back into interstellar space, cut off from the major source of its warmth by the ultimate, threatening blackness of Aidregh's world.

'But what,' Aidregh said steadily into the deepening gloom, 'what have you given me? You are sending me home with a gift that no man on my planet can resist. You have taught me nothing of the principles involved; you have given me only the smallest of clues which might lead me, or men much more intelligent than I, to the *voisk* forces which you value above all others. I know that we have centuries of new learning to encompass before we begin to know what the *voisk* spectrum might be like.

'In the meantime, you have given me a trick. You have given a savage a force that no one of his fellows can resist, and sent him irresponsibly home to play with it – or make himself king of his world with it. You have done this to preserve your own safety. How long will you be safe while savages play with the *voisk* force? *How long will you be safe from me?*'

No one moved. The darkness grew; neither the red sun nor the white could pass the high ramparts of the amphitheatre.

The Soul and the Breath were gone, and the Mind was going. Aidregh, even as he spoke, could remember nothing but himself as a twelve-year-old cadet, cut off from civilization with a small squad in a forest, minding a water-cooled searchlight. They had left the light pointing at the sky while they had cooked their field rations, and when they had come back to it, two hours later, the water in the cooling coils had been frozen solid – all its latent heat radiated off from the paraboloid mirror into Nowhere. That had been his first contact with deep space, right on the earth of his own land of Thrennen; and now he was standing at the focus of another, vaster mirror, while the blackness spread above it . . .

'You may well fear me,' he said into the total night. 'With the gift you have taught me to use, I can be more dangerous to you than my whole planet was, when we had nothing with which to threaten you but bombs. Your only hope, now, is to co-operate with us to the fullest. You will never again feel safe in confining any man from Home here while you teach him certain minor tricks. The floodgates are open. The flood will follow.

'But I will make you one promise, which I owe you for all the damage we have already done. The promise is this: After I have swayed my people away from this war, I shall resign. No politician should use the trick you have taught me more than once, and then only for what he believes to be an ultimate cause.

'But I shall not promise to refrain from using the trick again. I will use it. I will spend the rest of my life using it – but not as First Minister of Thrennen.

'This I promise, and that I say I will not promise. You have heard me. I have done more than try to sway you by the trick you taught me. I have told you what I intend. I have nothing more to say; judge now, Rathemen.'

He stood in the utter darkness on the stone, without a single star over him. The intangible, inaudible stress in the air was still growing, swelling to some crescendo he would never understand—

And then, just like that, it was gone. A thin, silvery veil of the Cluster peered wanly into the crater.

The stone benches were empty.

He had lost his audience – lost it as no man in history had ever lost an audience before. Of all that vast congregation, no one was left but Dr Ni and the children. No, there was one other group, far away along the stony reaches, but they were Homemen too – the crew, evidently.

Aidregh felt his knees buckling. Somehow, Ni got to him before he hit the ground beneath the white stone.

'Aidregh! What's the matter? Was it so hard? Corlant, Aidresne, quick. He's as limp as a rag. Aidregh, we're all here . . . it's all over . . . you did it, you did it. The war is over . . . it's over, can't you hear me?'

'I hear you,' Aidregh said, groping to a sitting position. 'But— It's over? They're gone! They didn't stay to listen! Ni, Ni, we've got to get away somehow . . . the bombs will be arriving in a few hours—'

'No, no, Aidregh. We're free. That's why the Rathemen are gone. The whole crew is here. We can go – and you did it.'

'We're already sending notice of our release to Signath,' Corlant said. She was kneeling beside him, her eyes brimming with tears. Aidresne stood over them both; looking both solemn and proud. 'You didn't see Margent when the light first began to come back. He bowed to you. They all did. And then they all flicked out like a light – they gave us our freedom, by leaving us alone.'

Aidregh stood up unsteadily, feeling his son's solid forearm rock-steady under his own. Ni was already leading the way up the nearest aisle, out of the vast deserted crater.

Outside the walls, the shadow of the amphitheatre's ramparts was being thrown across the gleaming desert by the setting Cluster. A phalanx of jointed groundcars was drawn up on the salt flats of some old sea, and from them Aidregh could hear a susurrus of voices speaking in the accents of Home: his crewmen, waiting. He began to hurry.

'Aidregh?' a voice said from behind him.

'Yes, Ni.'

'What now?'

'Deal with Signath,' Aidregh said.

'Yes, but then? Do you really mean to give up the Ministry?'

'Yes,' Aidregh said happily, rounding a sharp turn in the path by vaulting over a boulder. 'I'm going to try something new. I won't dare be a politician any longer – I'd be a monster in nothing flat. I'm going to strike out for myself.'

'How?' Ni demanded.

Aidregh stopped at the bottom of the winding path and looked out towards the waiting cars. Corlant took his hand, and Aidresne took hers.

'Wait and see,' he said; and suddenly they were running, all three, whooping with joy, along the salt flats towards Home. He stood for a moment and looked after them, shaking his head, and then broke into a reluctant dogtrot.

It was like a kind of dance, with the sighs and shouts and drumming feet of the crowd for music. On the platform, far away at the centre of the huge pavilion, Aidregh moved from one edge of the boards to another with desperation, his legs moving loosely, his arms, flapping, the white blur of his face turned appealingly to the tented sky and then to the swaying audience.

Corlant and Aidresne could hear his voice, but not what

he was saying. Only the wavering sound of someone shouting penetrated this far through the sea-roar of the crowd.

Aidregh fell on his knees at one border of the stage and held out his arms. A great groan of orgiastic sorrow spread from the people closest to that side of the platform, beating its way outwards through the pavilion like a wave of contagion. It was still coming towards Corlant and Aidresne like a foaming comber when Aidregh was on his feet again, striding towards the tent's centre pole, his fist raised at the pole, and then at the sky. After a moment's hesitation – which compelled instant silence at the centre of the audience – he rushed on to seize the ridgepole itself, in what was apparently an insane effort to wrest the immense duralumin mast bodily out of the ground.

The whole crowd was on its feet in an instant, screaming:

Get out of our sky! Get out—

On the stage, Aidregh clutched at the mast and turned slowly, looking out at the roaring mass of voices and fists. His face was blank, except for a small black O *where his mouth should have been, but it was perfectly plain what his stance meant. The words of the chant seemed to drive him back like blows, until he was standing only with the greatest effort.*

The chant began to falter. Aidregh's head was resting against the ridgepole, rocking a little as though every shout was a slap. His whole body was doing a dance of torture, and yet at the same time it did not seem to be moving. A horrified Ahhhhh! *rose into the middle of the chant and broke its rhythm; it died away rapidly. In the silence, someone began to weep.*

Aidregh had tempted them, and they had fallen. The old orgy of fury against the sky had broken out again, only because he had called it to their memories. Now they saw what their passion had cost them. The air of the pavilion was thick with shame.

The First Minister of Thrennen and his bride sat down, clinging to each other. They had not yet heard one intelligible word from Aidregh, but he had already wrung them dry – and knowing, approximately, how he was doing it seemed to be no protection. He straightened himself against the ridgepole with great effort, and the pole seemed to stiffen with him, as though it were once more ready to undertake its immemorial task of holding up the familiar sky. He came forward with slow painful steps, lifted his faraway face – and looked directly into their eyes.

In the intent hush, he began to speak. Now they could hear the familiar voice, saying unfamiliar, mystical things, as befitted the Prophet of Rathe. But they knew that it was speaking to them.

'Children— There is still time—'

And indeed there was. Aidregh had made it for them, and, as the Prophet of Rathe, was in the process of making more. The new worship of the sister planet had already ousted Cluster-worship, and had become central in the doctrines of astrology. It took hold wherever Aidregh spoke.

'There is still time,' he said. The congregation listened. 'Here is where we and the grass grow up, like music.'

I would most like to preface this story with the remarks made about it by Mr John Ciardi in a 1952 volume called Witches Three, *but unhappily Mr Ciardi's discussion ran for six long paragraphs, or five more than I can allow here. Fundamentally, the American poet saw in the pages which follow a parable of the guilt witch, who in a symbolic dance of self-extermination washes out our guilt for having tried to interfere with nature (through the sorcerer, the scientist, or similar figure, called by Mr Ciardi 'the rain-plumber'). He sees Jarmoskowski as the black witch or rain-plumber, Doris as the blonde witch or good fairy, and concludes:* 'The good fairy and the witch want to destroy one another knowing that in so doing they will destroy themselves. *They want to be rid of the whole problem and of each other. They want Nirvana. They seek to end where all metaphysical wrestling seeks to end – in exhaustion and surrender.' If you find all this disquieting, however, rest one hand on the light-switch and repeat after me:*

There Shall Be No Darkness

I

It was about 10.00 p.m. when Paul Foote decided that there was a monster at Newcliffe's houseparty.

Foote was tight at the time – tighter than he liked to be ever. He sprawled in a too-easy chair in the front room, slanted on the end of his spine, his forearms resting on the high arms of the chair. A half-empty glass depended laxly from his right hand. A darker spot on one grey trouser-leg showed where some of the drink had gone. Through half-shut eyes he watched Jarmoskowski at the piano.

The pianist was playing, finally, his transcription of the Wolf's-Glen scene from von Weber's *Der Freischütz*. Though it was a tremendous technical showpiece, Jarmoskowski never used it in concert, but only at social gatherings. He played it with an odd, detached amusement which only made more astounding the way the notes came swarming out of Newcliffe's big Baldwin; the rest of the gathering had been waiting for it all evening.

For Foote, who was a painter with a tin ear, it wasn't music at all. It was an enormous, ominous noise, muted occasionally to allow the repetition of a cantrap whose implications were secret.

The room was stuffy and was only half as large as it had been during the afternoon, and Foote was afraid that he was the only living man in it except for Jan Jarmoskowski. The rest of the party were wax figures, pretending to be humans in an aesthetic trance.

Of Jarmoskowski's vitality there could be no question. He was not handsome, but there was in him a pure brute force that had its own beauty – that and the beauty of precision with which the force was controlled. When his big hairy hands came down it seemed that the piano should fall into flinders. But the impact of fingers upon keys was calculated to the single dyne.

It was odd to see such delicacy behind such a face. Jarmoskowski's hair grew too long on his rounded head, despite the fact that he had avoided carefully any suggestion of Musician's Haircut. His brows were straight, rectangular, so shaggy that they seemed to meet over his high-bridged nose.

From where Foote sat he noticed for the first time the odd

way the Pole's ears were placed – tilted forward as if in animal attention, so that the vestigial 'point' really was in the uppermost position. They were cocked directly towards the keyboard, reminding Foote irresistibly of the dog on the His Master's Voice trade-mark.

Where had he seen that head before? In Matthias Gruenewald, perhaps – in that panel on the Isenheim Altar that showed the Temptation of St Anthony. Or had it been in one of the illustrations in the *Red Grimoire*, those dingy, primitive woodcuts which Chris Lundgren called 'Rorschak tests of the medieval mind?'

On a side-table next to the chair the painter's cigarette burned in an onyx ashtray which bore also a tiny dancer frozen in twisted metal. From the unlit end of the cigarette a small tendril of white smoke flowed downwards and oozed out into a clinging pool, an amoeboid blur against the dark mahogany. The river of sound subsided suddenly and the cantrap was spoken, the three even, stony syllables and the answering wail. The pool of smoke leapt up in the middle exactly as if something had been dropped into it. Then the piano was howling again under Jarmoskowski's fingers, and the tiny smoke-spout twisted in the corner of Foote's vision, becoming more and more something like the metal dancer. His mouth dry, Foote shifted to the outer edge of the chair.

The transcription ended with three sharp chords, a 'concert ending' contrived to suggest the three plucked notes of the cantrap. The smoke-figurine toppled and slumped as if stabbed; it poured over the edge of the table and disintegrated swiftly on the air. Jarmoskowski paused, touched his finger-tips together reflectively, and then began a work more purely his own: the *Galliard Fantasque*.

The wax figures did not stir, but a soft eerie sigh of recognition came from their frozen lips. Through the window behind the pianist a newly risen moon showed another petrified vista, the snowy expanse of Newcliffe's Scottish estate.

There was another person in the room, but Foote could not tell who it was. When he turned his unfocused eyes to count, his mind went back on him and he never managed to reach a total; but somehow there was the impression of another presence that had not been of the party before. Someone Tom and Caroline hadn't invited was sitting in. Not Doris, nor Palmer, the Labour MP, either; they were too simple. By the same token, Bennington, the American critic, was much too tubbily comfortable to have standing as a menace. The visiting psychiatrist, Lundgren, Foote had known well in Sweden, and Hermann Ehrenberg was only another refugee novelist and didn't count; for that matter, no novelist was worth a snap in a painter's universe, so that crossed out Alec James, too.

His glance moved of itself back to the composer. Jarmoskowski was not the presence. He had been there before. But he had something to do with it. There was an eleventh presence now, and it had something to do with Jarmoskowski.

What was it?

For it was there – there was no doubt about that. The energy which the rest of Foote's senses ordinarily would have consumed was flowing into his instincts now, because his senses were numbed. Acutely, poignantly, his instincts told him of the monster. It hovered around the piano, sat next to Jarmoskowski as he caressed the musical beast's teeth, blended with the long body and the serpentine fingers.

Foote had never had the horrors from drinking before, and he knew he did not have them now. A part of his mind which was not drunk and could never be drunk had recognized real horror somewhere in the room; and the whole of his mind, its barriers of scepticism tumbled, believed and trembled within itself.

The batlike circling of the frantic notes was stilled abruptly. Foote blinked, startled.

'Already?' he said stupidly.

'Already?' Jarmoskowski echoed. 'But that's a long piece, Paul. Your fascination speaks well for my writing.'

His eyes turned directly upon the painter; they were almost completely suffused, though Jarmoskowski never drank. Foote tried frantically to remember whether or not his eyes had been red during the afternoon, and whether it was possible for any man's eyes to be as red at any time as this man's were now.

'The writing?' he said, condensing the far-flung diffusion of his brain. Newcliffe's highballs were damn strong. 'Hardly the writing, Jan. Such fingers as those could put fascination into "Three Blind Mice".'

He snickered inside at the parade of emotions which marched across Jarmoskowski's face: startlement at a compliment from Foote – for the painter had a reputation for a savage tongue, and the inexplicable antagonism which had arisen between the two since the pianist had first arrived had given Foote plenty of opportunity to justify it – then puzzled reflection – and then at last veiled anger as the hidden slur bared its fangs in his mind. Nevertheless the man could laugh at it.

'They are long, aren't they?' he said to the rest of the group, unrolling the fingers like the party noisemakers which turn from snail to snake when blown through. 'But it's a mistake to suppose that they assist my playing, I assure you. Mostly they stumble over each other. Especially over this one.'

He held up his hands for inspection. On both, the index fingers and the middle fingers were exactly the same length.

'I suppose Lundgren would call me a mutation,' Jarmoskowski said. 'It's a nuisance at the piano. I have to work out my own fingerings for everything, even the simplest pieces.'

Doris Gilmore, once a student of Jarmoskowski's in Prague, and still obviously, painfully in love with him, shook coppery hair back from her shoulders and held up her own hands.

'My fingers are so stubby,' she said ruefully. 'Hardly pianist's hands at all.'

'On the contrary – the hands of a master pianist,' Jarmoskowski said. He smiled, scratching his palms abstractedly, and Foote found himself in a universe of brilliant, perfectly even teeth. No, not perfectly even. The polished rows were bounded almost mathematically by slightly longer canines. They reminded him of that idiotic Poe story – was it *Berenice*? Obviously Jarmoskowski would not die a natural death. He would be killed by a dentist for possession of those teeth.

'Three-fourths of the greatest pianists I know have hands like truck drivers,' Jarmoskowski was saying, 'Surgeons too, as Lundgren will tell you. Long fingers tend to be clumsy.'

'You seem to manage to make tremendous music, all the same,' Newcliffe said, getting up.

'Thank you, Tom.' Jarmoskowski seemed to take his host's rising as a signal that he was not going to be required to play any more. He lifted his feet from the pedals and swung them around to the end of the bench. Several of the others rose also. Foote struggled up on to numb feet from the infernal depths of the armchair. Setting his glass on the side-table a good distance away from the onyx ashtray, he picked his way cautiously over to Christian Lundgren.

'Chris, I'm a fan of yours,' he said, controlling his tongue with difficulty. 'Now I'm sorry. I read your paper, the one you read to the Stockholm Endo-crin-ological Congress. Aren't Jarmoskowski's hands—'

'Yes, they are,' the psychiatrist said, looking at Foote with sharp, troubled eyes. Suddenly Foote was aware of Lundgren's chain of thought; he knew the scientist very well. The grey, craggy man was assessing Foote's drunkenness, and wondering whether or not he would have forgotten the whole affair in the morning.

Lundgren made a gesture of dismissal. 'I saw them too,' he said, his tone flat. 'A mutation, probably, as he himself suggested. Not every woman with a white streak through her hair is a witch; I give Jan the same reservation.'

'That's not all, Chris.'

'It is all I need to consider, since I live in the twentieth century. I am going to bed and forget all about it. Which you may take for advice as well as for information, Paul, if you will.'

He stalked out of the room, leaving Foote standing alone, wondering whether to be reassured or more alarmed than before. Lundgren should know, and certainly the platinum path which parted Doris Gilmore's absurdly red hair indicated nothing about Doris but that her coiffure was too chic for her young, placid face. But Jarmoskowski was not so simple; if he was despite Lundgren just what he seemed—

The party appeared to be surviving quite nicely without Foote, or Lundgren either. Conversations were starting up about the big room. Jarmoskowski and Doris shared the piano bench and were talking in low tones, punctuated now and then by brilliant bits of passage work; evidently the Pole was showing her better ways of handling the Hindemith sonata she had played before dinner. James and Ehrenberg were dissecting each other's most recent books with civilized savagery before a fascinated Newcliffe. Blandly innocent Caroline Newcliffe was talking animatedly to Bennington and Palmer about nothing at all. Nobody missed Lundgren, and it seemed even less likely that Foote would be missed.

He walked with wobbly nonchalance into the dining-room, where the butler was still clearing the table.

' 'Scuse me,' he said. 'Little experiment, if y'don't mind. Return it in the morning.' He snatched a knife from the table, looked for the door which led directly from the dining-room into the foyer, propelled himself through it. The hallway was dim, but intelligible; so was the talk in the next room.

As he passed the French door, he saw Bennington's figure through the ninon marquisette, now standing by the piano watching the progress of the lesson. The critic's voice stopped him dead as he was sliding the knife into his jacket. Foote was an incurable eavesdropper.

'Hoofy's taken his head to bed,' Bennington was remarking. 'I'm rather relieved. I thought he was going to be more unpleasant than he was.'

'What was the point of that fuss about the silverware, at dinner?' the girl said. 'Is he noted for that sort of thing?'

'Somewhat. He's really quite a brilliant artist, but being years ahead of one's time is frequently hard on the temper.'

'He had me worried,' Jarmoskowski confessed. 'He kept looking at me as if I had forgotten to play the repeats.'

Bennington chuckled. 'In the presence of another inarguable artist he seems to become very malignant. You were being flattered, Jan.'

Foote's attention was attracted by a prodigious yawn from Palmer. The MP was showing his preliminary signals of boredom, and at any moment now would break unceremoniously for his bed. Reluctantly Foote resumed his arrested departure; still the conversations babbled on indifferently behind him. The corners of his mouth pulled down, he passed the stairway and on down the hall.

As he swung closed the door of his bedroom, he paused a moment to listen to Jarmoskowski's technical exhibition on the keys, the only sound from the living-room which was still audible at this distance. Then he shut the door all the way with a convulsive shrug. Let them say about Foote what they liked, even if it sometimes had to be the truth; but nevertheless it might be that at midnight Jarmoskowski would give another sort of exhibition.

If he did, Foote would be glad to have the knife.

II

At 11.30, Jarmoskowski stood alone on the terrace of Newcliffe's country house. Although there was no wind, the night was frozen with a piercing cold – but he did not seem to notice it. He stood motionless, like a black statue, with only the long streamers of his breathing, like twin jets of steam from the nostrils of a dragon, to show that he was alive.

Through the haze of watered silk which curtained Foote's window, Jarmoskowski was an heroic pillar of black stone – a pillar above a fumarole.

The front of the house was evidently entirely dark: there was no light on the pianist's back or shoulders. He was silhouetted against the snow, which gleamed dully in the moonlight. The shadow of the heavy tower which was the house's axis looked like a donjonkeep. Thin slits of embrasures, Foote remembered, watched the landscape with a dark vacuity, and each of the crowning merlons wore a helmet of snow.

He could feel the house huddling against the malice of the white Scottish night. A sense of age invested it. The curtains smelled of dust and spices. It seemed impossible that anyone but Foote and Jarmoskowski could be alive in it.

After a long moment, Foote moved the curtain very slightly and drew it back. His face was drenched in reflected moonlight and he stepped back into the dark again, leaving the curtains parted.

If Jarmoskowski saw the furtive movement he gave no sign. He remained engrossed in the acerb beauty of the night. Almost the whole of Newcliffe's estate was visible from where he stood. Even the black border of the forest, beyond the golf-course to the right, could be seen through the dry frigid air. A few isolated trees stood nearer the house, casting sharply etched shadows on the snow, shadows that flowed and changed shape with the slow movement of the moon.

Jarmoskowski sighed and scratched his left palm. His lips moved soundlessly.

A cloud floated across the moon, its shadow preceding it, gliding in a rush of ink athwart the house. The gentle ripples of the snow-field reared ahead of the wave, like breakers, falling back, engulfed, then surging again much closer. A thin singing of wind rose briefly, whirling crystalline showers of snow from the terrace flagstones.

The wind died as the umbra engulfed the house. For a long instant, the darkness and silence persisted. Then, from somewhere near the stables and greenhouses behind the house, a dog raised his voice in a faint sustained throbbing howl. Others joined in.

Jarmoskowski's teeth gleamed in the occluded moonlight. He stood a moment longer; then his head turned with a quick jerk and his eyes flashed a feral scarlet at the dark window where Foote hovered. Foote released the curtains hastily. Even through them he could see the pianist's phosphorescent smile.

The dog keened again. Jarmoskowski went back into the

house. Foote scurried to his door and cocked one eye around the jamb.

Some men, as has somewhere been remarked, cannot pass a bar; some cannot pass a woman; some cannot pass a rare stamp or a good fire. Foote could not help spying, but in this one case he knew that one thing could be said for him: *this* time he wanted to be in the wrong.

There was a single small light burning in the corridor. Jarmoskowski's room was at the end of the hall, next to Foote's. As the pianist walked reflectively towards it, the door of the room directly across from Foote's swung open and Doris Gilmore came out, clad in a quilted sapphire housecoat with a high Russian collar. The effect was marred a little by the towel over her arm and the toothbrush in her hand, but nevertheless she looked startlingly pretty.

'Oh!' she said. Jarmoskowski turned towards her, and then neither of them said anything for a while.

Foote ground his teeth. Was the girl, too, to be a witness to the thing he expected from Jarmoskowski? That would be beyond all decency. And it must be nearly midnight now.

The two still had not moved. Trembling, Foote edged out into the hall and slid behind Jarmoskowski's back along the wall to Jarmoskowski's room. By the grace of God, the door was open.

In a quieter voice, Doris said, 'Oh, it's you, Jan. You startled me.'

'So I see. I'm most sorry,' Jarmoskowski's voice said. Foote again canted his head until he could see them both. 'It appears that we are the night-owls of the party.'

'I think the rest are tight. Especially that horrible painter. I've been reading the magazines Tom left by my bed, and I finally decided I'd better try to sleep too. What have you been up to?'

'I was out on the terrace, getting a breath. I like the winter night – it bites.'

'The dogs are restless, too,' she said. 'Did you hear them? I suppose Brucey started them off.'

Jarmoskowski smiled. 'Very likely. Why does a full moon make a dog feel so sorry for himself?'

'Maybe there's a banshee about.'

'I doubt it,' Jarmoskowski said. 'This house isn't old enough to have any family psychopomps; it's massive, but largely imitation. And as far as I know, none of Tom's or Caroline's relatives have had the privilege of dying in it.'

'Don't. You talk as if you believed it.' She wrapped the housecoat tighter about her waist; Foote guessed that she was repressing a shiver.

'I came from a country where belief in such things is common. In Poland most sceptics are imported.'

'I wish you'd pretend to be an exception,' she said. 'You're giving me the creeps, Jan.'

He nodded seriously. 'That's – fair enough,' he said gently.

There was another silence, while they looked at each other anew in the same dim light. Then Jarmoskowski stepped forward and took her hands in his.

Foote felt a long-belated flicker of embarrassment. Nothing could be more normal than this, and nothing interested him less. He was an eavesdropper, not a voyeur. If he were wrong after all, he'd speedily find himself in a position for which no apology would be possible.

The girl was looking up at Jarmoskowski, smiling uncertainly. Her smile was so touching as to make Foote writhe inside his skin. 'Jan,' she said.

'No . . . Doris, wait,' Jarmoskowski said indistinctly. 'Wait just a moment. It has been a long time since Prague.'

'I see,' she said. She tried to release her hands.

Jarmoskowski said sharply: 'You don't see. I was eighteen then. You were – what was it? – eleven, I think. In those days I was proud of your schoolgirl crush, but of course infinitely too old for you. I am not so old any more, and when I saw this afternoon how lovely you have become the years went away like dandelion-fluff – no, no, hear me out, please! There is much more. I love you now, Doris, as I can see you love me; but—'

In the brief pause Foote could hear the sharp indrawn breaths that Doris was trying to control. He felt like crawling. He had no business—

'But we must wait a little, Doris. I know something that concerns you that you do not know yourself. And I must warn you of something in Jan Jarmoskowski that neither of us could even have dreamed in the old days.'

'Warn – me?'

'Yes.' Jarmoskowski paused again. Then he said: 'You will find it hard to believe. But if you can, we may be happy. Doris, I cannot be a sceptic. I am—'

He stopped. He had looked down abstractedly at her hands, as if searching for precisely the right English words. Then, slowly, he turned her hands over until they rested palms up on his. An expression of absolute shock transformed his face, and Foote saw his grip tighten spasmodically.

In that tetanic silence Foote heard his judgment of Jarmoskowski confirmed. It gave him no pleasure. He was frightened.

For an instant Jarmoskowski shut his eyes. The muscles along his jaw stood out with the violence with which he was clenching his teeth. Then, deliberately, he folded Doris's hands together, and his curious fingers made a fist about them. When his eyes opened again they were as red as flame in the weak light.

Doris jerked her hands free and crossed them over her breasts. 'Jan – Jan, what is it? What's the matter?'

His face, that should have been flying into flinders under the force of the knowledge behind it, came under control muscle by muscle.

'Nothing,' he said. 'There's really no point in what I was going to say. I have been foolish; please pardon me. Nice to have seen you again, Doris. Good night.'

He brushed past her and stalked on down the corridor. Doris turned to look after him, her cheeks beginning to glisten, one freed hand clutching her toothbrush.

Jarmoskowski wrenched the unresisting doorknob of his room and threw the door shut behind him. Foote only barely managed to dodge out of his way.

Behind the house, a dog howled and went silent again.

III

In Jarmoskowski's room the moonlight played in through the open window upon a carefully turned-down bed. The cold air had penetrated every cranny. He ran both hands through his hair and went directly across the carpet to the table beside his bed. As he crossed the path of colourless light his shadow was oddly foreshortened, so that it looked as if he were walking on all fours. There was a lamp on the side-table and he reached for it.

Then he stopped dead still, his hand half-way to the switch. He seemed to be listening. Finally, he turned and looked back across the room, directly at the spot behind the door where Foote was standing.

It was the blackest spot of all, for it had its back to the moon; but Jarmoskowski said immediately, 'Hello, Paul. Aren't you up rather late?'

Foote did not reply for a while. His senses were still alcohol-numbed, and he was further poisoned by the sheer outrageous impossibility of the thing he knew to be true. He stood silently in the darkness, watching the Pole's barely visible figure beside the fresh bed, and the sound of his own breathing was loud in his ears. The broad flat streamer of moonlight lay between them like a metallic river.

'I'm going to bed shortly,' he said at last. His voice sounded flat and dead and faraway, as if it belonged to someone else entirely. 'I just came to issue a little warning.'

'Well, well,' said Jarmoskowski pleasantly. 'Warnings seem to be all the vogue this evening. Do you customarily pay your social calls with a knife in your hand?'

'That's the warning, Jarmoskowski. The knife. I'm sleeping with it. It's made of silver.'

'You must be drunker than usual,' said the composer. 'Why don't you just go to bed – with the knife, if you fancy it? We can talk again in the morning.'

'Don't give me that,' Foote snapped savagely. 'You can't fool me. I know you for what you are.'

'All right, you know me. Is it a riddle? I'll bite, as Bennington would say.'

'Yes, you'd bite,' Foote said, and his voice shook a little despite himself. 'Should I really give it a name, Jarmoskowski? Where you were born it was *vrolok*, wasn't it? And in France it was *loup-garou*. In the Carpathians it was *stregoica* or *strega*, or sometimes *vlkoslak*. In—'

'Your command of languages is greater than your common sense,' Jarmoskowski said. 'And *stregoica* and *strega* are different in sex, and neither of them is equivalent to *loup-garou*. But all the same you interest me. Isn't it a little out of season for all such things? Wolfbane does not bloom in the dead of winter. And perhaps the things you give so many fluent names are also out of season in 1952.'

'The dogs hate you,' Foote said softly. 'That was a fine display Brucey put on this afternoon, when Tom brought him in from his run and he found you here. I doubt that you've forgotten it. I think you've seen a dog behave like that before, walking sideways through a room where you were, growling, watching you with every step until Tom or some other owner dragged him out. He's howling now.

'And that shock you got from the table silverware at dinner – and your excuse about rubber-soled shoes. I looked under the table, if you recall, and your shoes turned out to be leather-soled. But it was a pretty feeble excuse anyhow, for anybody knows that you can't get an electric shock from an ungrounded piece of tableware, no matter how long you've been scuffing rubber. Silver's deadly, isn't it, Jarmoskowski?

'And those fingers – the index fingers as long as the middle ones – you were clever about those. You were careful to call everybody's attention to them. It's supposed to be the obvious that everybody misses. But Jarmoskowski, that "Purloined Letter" mechanism has been ground through too often already in detective stories. It didn't fool Lundgren, it didn't fool me.'

'Ah, so,' Jarmoskowski said. 'Quite a catalogue.'

'There's more. How does it happen that your eyes were grey all afternoon, and turned red as soon as the moon rose? And the palms of your hands – there was some hair growing there, but you shaved it off, didn't you, Jarmoskowski? I've been watching you scratch them. Everything about you, the way you look, the way you talk, every move you make – it all screams out your nature in a dozen languages to anyone who knows the signs.'

After a long silence, Jarmoskowski said, 'I see. You've been most attentive, Paul – I see you are what people call the suspicious drunk. But I appreciate your warning, Paul. Let us suppose that what you say of me is true. What then?

Are you prepared to broadcast it to the rest of the house? Would you like to be known until the day you die as "The Boy Who Cried–" '

'I don't intend to say anything unless you make it necessary. I want you to know that I know, in case you've seen a pentagram on anyone's palm tonight.'

Jarmoskowski smiled. 'Have you thought that, knowing that you know, I could have no further choice? That the first word you said to me about it all might brand *your* palm with the pentagram?'

Foote had not thought about it. He had spent far too much time convincing himself that it had all come out of the bottle. He heard the silver knife clatter against the floor before he was aware that he had dropped it; his eyes throbbed with the effort to see through the dimness the hands he was holding before them.

From the other side of his moonlit room, Jarmoskowski's voice drifted, dry, distant, and amused. 'So – you hadn't thought. That's too bad. *Better never* than late, Paul.'

The dim figure of Jarmoskowski began to sink down, rippling a little in the reflected moonlight. At first it seemed only as if he were sitting down upon the bed; but the foreshortening proceeded without any real movement, and the pianist's body was twisting, too, and his clothing with it, his shirt-bosom dimming to an indistinct blaze upon his broadening chest, his shoulders hunching, his pointed jaw already squared into a blunt muzzle, his curled pads ticking as they struck the bare floor and moved deliberately towards Foote. His tail was thrust straight out behind him, and the ruff of coarse hair along his back stirred gently. He sniffed.

Somehow Foote got his legs to move. He found the doorknob and threw himself out of Jarmoskowski's room into the corridor.

A bare second after he had slammed the door, something

struck it a massive blow from inside. The panelling split sharply. He held it shut by the knob with all the strength in his body. He could see almost nothing; his eyes seemed to have rolled all the way back into his head.

A dim white shape drifted down upon him through the dark corridor, and a fresh spasm of fear sent rivers of sweat down his back, his sides, his cheeks. But it was only the girl.

'Paul! What on Earth! What's the *matter*?'

'Quick!' he said, choking. 'Get something silver – something heavy made out of silver – quick, *quick*!'

Despite her astonishment, the frantic urgency in his voice drove her away. She darted back into her room. Kalpas of eternity went by after that while he listened for sounds inside Jarmoskowski's room. Once he thought he heard a low rumble, but he was not sure. The sea-like hissing and sighing of his blood, rushing through the channels of the middle ear, seemed very loud to him. He couldn't imagine why it was not arousing the whole countryside. He clung to the doorknob and panted.

Then the girl was back, bearing a silver candlestick nearly three feet in length – a weapon that was almost too good, for his fright-weakened muscles had some difficulty in lifting it. He shifted his grip on the knob to the left hand alone, and hefted the candlestick awkwardly with his right.

'All right,' he said, in what he hoped was a grim voice. 'Now let him come.'

'What in heaven's name is this all about?' Doris said. 'You're waking everybody in the house with this racket. Look – even the dog's come in to see—'

'The dog!'

He swung around, releasing the doorknob. Not ten paces from them, an enormous coal-black animal, nearly five feet in length, grinned at them with polished fangs. As soon as it saw Foote move it snarled. Its eyes gleamed red under the single bulb.

It sprang.

Foote heaved the candlestick high and brought it down – but the animal was not there. Somehow the leap was never completed. There was a brief flash of movement at the open end of the corridor, then darkness and silence.

'He saw the candlestick,' Foote panted. 'Must have jumped out the window and come around through the front door. Then he saw the silver and beat it.'

'Paul!' Doris cried. 'What – how did you know that thing would jump? It was so big! And what has silver—'

He chuckled, surprising even himself. He had a mental picture of what the truth was going to sound like to Doris. 'That,' he said, 'was a wolf and a whopping one. Even the usual kind isn't very friendly and—'

Footsteps sounded on the floor above, and the voice of Newcliffe, grumbling loudly, came down the stairs. Newcliffe liked his evenings noisy and his nights quiet. The whole house now seemed to have heard the commotion, for in a moment a number of half-clad figures were elbowing out into the corridor, wanting to know what was up or plaintively requesting less noise.

Abruptly the lights went on, revealing blinking faces and pyjama-clad forms struggling into robes. Newcliffe came down the stairs. Caroline was with him, impeccable even in disarray, her face openly and honestly ignorant and unashamedly beautiful. She was no lion-hunter but she loved parties. Evidently she was pleased that the party was starting again.

'What's all this?' Newcliffe demanded in a gravelly voice. 'Foote, are you the centre of this whirlpool? Why all the noise?'

'Werewolf,' Foote said, as painfully conscious as he had expected to be of how meaningless the word would sound. 'We've got a werewolf here. And somebody's marked out for him.'

How else could you put it? Let it stand.

There was a chorus of 'What's' as the group jostled about him. 'Eh? What was it? . . . Werewolf, I thought he said . . . What's this all about? . . . Somebody's been a wolf . . . Is that new? . . . What an uproar!'

'Paul,' Lundgren's voice cut through. 'Details, please.'

'Jarmoskowski's a werewolf,' Foote said grimly, making his tone as emotionless and factual as he could. 'I suspected it earlier tonight and went into his room and accused him of it. He changed shape, right on the spot while I was watching.'

The sweat started out afresh at the recollection of that half-seen mutation. 'He came around into the hall and went for us. I scared him off with a silver candlestick for a club.' He realized that he still held the candlestick and brandished it as proof. 'Doris saw the wolf – she'll vouch for that.'

'I saw a big dog-like thing, all right,' Doris admitted. 'And it did jump at us. It was black and had a lot of teeth. But – Paul, was that supposed to be Jan? Why, that's ridiculous.'

'It certainly is,' Newcliffe said feelingly. 'Getting us all up for a practical joke. Probably one of the dogs is loose.'

'Do you have any all-black dogs five feet long?' Foote demanded desperately. 'And where's Jarmoskowski now? Why isn't he here? Answer me that!'

Bennington gave a sceptical grunt from the background and opened Jarmoskowski's door. The party tried to jam itself as a unit into the room. Foote forced his way through the clot.

'See? He isn't here, either. And the bed's not been slept in. Doris—' He paused for an instant, realizing what he was about to admit, then plunged ahead. The stakes were now too big to hesitate over social conventions. 'Doris, you saw him go in here. Did you see him come out again?'

The girl looked startled. 'No, but I was in my room—'

'All right. Here. Look at this.' Foote led the way over to the window and pointed out. 'See? The prints on the snow?'

One by one the others leaned out. There was no arguing it. A set of animal prints, like large dog-tracks, led away from a spot just beneath Jarmoskowski's window – a spot where the disturbed snow indicated the landing of some heavy body.

'Follow them around,' Foote said. 'They lead around to the front door, and away again – I hope.'

'Have you traced them?' James asked.

'I didn't have to. I saw the thing, James.'

'The tracks could be coincidence,' Caroline suggested. 'Maybe Jan just went for a walk.'

'Barefoot? There are his shoes.'

Bennington vaulted over the window-sill with an agility astonishing in so round a man, and ploughed away with slippered feet along the line of tracks. A little while later he entered the room behind their backs.

'Paul's right,' he said, above the hubbub of excited conversation. 'The tracks go around to the terrace to the front door, then away again and around the side of the house towards the golf-course.' He rolled up his wet pyjama-cuffs awkwardly. A little of the weight came off Foote's heart; at least the beast was not still in the house, then—

'This is crazy,' Newcliffe declared angrily. 'We're like a lot of little children, panicked by darkness. There's no such thing as a werewolf.'

'I wouldn't place any wagers on that,' Ehrenberg said. 'Millions of people have believed in the werewolf for hundreds of years. One multiplies the years by the people and the answer is a big figure, *nicht wahr*?'

Newcliffe turned sharply to Lundgren. 'Chris, I can depend upon you at least to have your wits about you.'

The psychiatrist smiled wanly. 'You didn't read my Stockholm paper, did you, Tom? I mean my paper on psychoses of Middle Age populations. Much of it dealt with lycanthropy – werewolfism.'

'You mean – you believe this idiot story?'

'I spotted Jarmoskowski early in the evening,' Lundgren said. 'He must have shaved the hair on his palms, but he has all the other signs – eyes bloodshot with moonrise, first and second fingers of equal length, pointed ears, merged eyebrows, domed prefrontal bones, elongated upper cuspids. In short, the typical hyperpineal type – a lycanthrope.'

'Why didn't you say something?'

'I have a natural horror of being laughed at,' Lundgren said dryly. 'And *I didn't want to draw Jarmoskowski's attention to me.* These endocrine-imbalance cases have a way of making enemies very easily.'

Foote grinned ruefully. If he had thought of that part of it before he had confronted Jarmoskowski, he would have kept his big mouth shut. It was deflating to know how ignoble one's motives could be in the face of the most demanding situations.

'Lycanthropy is no longer common,' Lundgren droned, 'and so seldom mentioned except in out-of-the-way journals. It is the little-known aberration of a little-known ductless gland; beyond that we know only what he knew in 1400, and that is that it appears to enable the victim to control his shape.'

'I'm still leery of this whole business,' Bennington growled, from somewhere deep in his teddy-bear chest. 'I've known Jan for years. Nice fella – helped me out of a bad hole once, without owing me any favours at all. And I think there's enough discord in this house so that I won't add to it much if I say I wouldn't trust Paul Foote as far as I could throw him. By God, Paul, if this does turn out to be some practical joke of yours—'

'Ask Lundgren,' Foote said.

There was dead silence, disturbed only by heavy breathing. Lundgren was known to almost all of them as the world's ultimate authority on hormone-created insanity. Nobody seemed to want to ask him.

'Paul's right,' Lundgren said at last. 'You must take it or leave it. Jarmoskowski is a lycanthrope. A hyperpineal. No other gland could affect the blood vessels of the eyes like that or make such a reorganization of the soma possible. Jarmoskowski is inarguably a werewolf.'

Bennington sagged, the light of righteous incredulity dying from his eyes. 'I'll be damned!' he muttered. 'It can't be. It can't be.'

'We've got to get him tonight,' Foote said. 'He's seen the pentagram on somebody's palm – somebody in the party.'

'What's that?' asked James.

'It's a five-pointed star inscribed in a circle, a very old magical symbol. You find it in all the old mystical books, right back to the so-called fourth and fifth Books of Moses. The werewolf sees it on the palm of his next victim.'

There was a gasping little scream from Doris. 'So that's it!' she cried. 'Dear God, I'm the one! He saw something on my hand tonight while we were talking in the hall. He was awfully startled and went away with hardly another word. He said he was going to warn me about something and then he—'

'Steady,' Bennington said, in a soft voice that had all the penetrating power of a thunderclap. 'There's safety in numbers. We're all here.' Nevertheless, he could not keep himself from glancing surreptitiously over his shoulder.

'It's a common illusion in lycanthropic seizures,' Lundgren agreed. 'Or hallucination, I should say. But Paul, you're wrong about its significance to the lycanthrope; I believe you must have got that idea from some movie. The pentagram means something quite different. Doris, let me ask you a question.'

'Why – certainly, Dr Lundgren. What is it?'

'What were you doing with that piece of modelling clay this evening?'

To Foote, and evidently to the rest of the party, the question was meaningless. Doris, however, looked down at the floor and scuffed one slippered toe back and forth over the carpet.

'Answer me, please,' Lundgren said patiently. 'I watched you manipulating it while Jan was playing, and it seemed to me to be an odd thing for a woman to have in her handbag. What were you doing with it?'

'I – was trying to scare Paul Foote,' she said, in so low a voice that she could scarcely be heard at all.

'How? Believe me, Doris, this is most important. How?'

'There was a little cloud of smoke coming out of his cigarette. I was – trying to make it take—'

'Yes. Go on.'

'—Take the shape of a statuette near it,' Foote said flatly. He could feel droplets of ice on his forehead. The girl looked at him sideways; then she nodded and looked back at the floor. 'The music helped,' she murmured.

'Very good,' Lundgren said. 'Doris, I'm not trying to put you on the spot. Have you had much success at this sort of game?'

'Lately,' she said, not quite so reluctantly. 'It doesn't always work. But sometimes it does.'

'Chris, what does this mean?' Foote demanded.

'It means that we have an important ally here, if only we can find out how to make use of her,' Lundgren said. 'This girl is what the Middle Ages would have called a witch. Nowadays we'd probably say she's been given a liberal helping of extra-sensory powers, but I must confess that never seems to me to explain much that the old term didn't explain.

'That is the significance of the pentagram, and Jarmoskowski knows it very well. The werewolf hunts best and ranges most widely when he has a witch for an accomplice, as a mate when they are both in human form, as a marker or stalker when the werewolf is in the animal form. The appearance of the pentagram identifies to the lycanthrope the witch he believes appointed for him.'

'That's hardly good news,' Doris said faintly.

'But it is. In all these ancient psychopathic relationships there is a natural – or, if you like, a supernatural – balance. The werewolf adopts such a partner with the belief – for him of course it is a certain foreknowledge – that the witch inevitably will betray him. That is what so shocked Jarmoskowski; but his changing to the wolf form shows that he has taken the gambit. He knows as well as we do, probably better, that as a witch Doris is only a beginner, unaware of most of her own powers. He is gambling very coolly on our being unable to use her against him. It is my belief that he is most wrong.'

'So we still don't know who Jan's chosen as a victim,' James said in earnest, squeaky tones. 'That settles it. We've got to trail the – the beast and kill him. We must kill him before he kills one of us – if not Doris, then somebody else. Even if he misses us, it would be just as bad to have him roaming the countryside.'

'What are you going to kill him with?' Lundgren asked matter-of-factly.

'Eh?'

'I said, what are you going to kill him with? With that pineal hormone in his blood he can laugh at any ordinary bullet. And since there are no chapels dedicated to St Hubert around here, you won't be able to scare him to death with a church-blessed bullet.'

'Silver will do,' Foote said.

'Yes, silver will do. It poisons the pinearin-catalysis. But are you going to hunt a full-grown wolf armed with table silver and candlesticks? Or is somebody here metallurgist enough to cast a decent silver bullet?'

Foote sighed. With the burden of proof lifted from him, and completely sobered up by shock, he felt a little more like his old self, despite the pall which hung over him and the others.

'Like I always tell my friends,' he said, 'there's never a dull moment at a Newcliffe house-party.'

IV

The clock struck 1.30. Foote picked up one of Newcliffe's rifles and hefted it. It felt – useless. He said, 'How are you coming?'

The group gathered together in one corner of the kitchen shook their heads in comical unison. They were trying to melt down some soft unalloyed silver articles, mostly of Mexican manufacture, with a blowtorch. The flame sent fantastic shadows shooting over their intent faces.

'We've got it melted, all right,' Bennington said, after a while, peering into the small earthenware bowl, also Mexican, which they were using as a crucible. 'But what do we do with it now? Drop it from the top of the tower?'

'You can't kill a wolf with buckshot unless you're damned lucky,' Newcliffe pointed out. Now that the problem had been reduced temporarily from a hypernatural one to a matter of ordinary hunting, he was in his element. 'And I haven't got a decent shotgun here anyhow. But we ought to be able to whack together a mould. The bullet should be soft enough so that it won't stick in the rifling of my guns.'

He opened the door to the cellar stairs and disappeared down them, carrying in one hand several ordinary rifle cartridges. Faintly, the dogs renewed their howling. Doris began to tremble. Foote put his arm around her.

'It's all right,' he said. 'We'll get him. You're safe enough.'

She swallowed. 'I know,' she agreed in a small voice. 'But every time I think of the way he looked at my hands, and how red his eyes were— You don't suppose he's prowling around the house? That that's what the dogs are howling about?'

'I don't know,' Foote said carefully. 'But dogs are funny that way. They can sense things at great distances. I suppose a man with pinearin in his blood would have a strong odour to them. But he probably knows that we're after his scalp, so he won't be hanging around if he's smart.'

She managed a tremulous smile. 'All right,' she said. 'I'll try not to be hysterical.' He gave her an awkward reassuring pat, feeling a little absurd.

'Do you suppose we can use the dogs?' Ehrenberg wanted to know.

'Certainly,' said Lundgren. 'Dogs have always been our greatest allies against the abnormal. You saw what a rage Jarmoskowski's very presence put Brucey in this afternoon. He must have smelled the incipient seizure. Ah, Tom – what did you manage?'

Newcliffe set a wooden transplanting box on the kitchen table. 'I pried the slug out of one shell for each gun,' he said, 'and used one of them to make impressions in the clay here.

The cold has made the stuff pretty hard, so the impressions should be passable moulds. Bring the silver over here.'

Bennington did as he was told.

'All right, pour,' Newcliffe said. 'Chris, you don't suppose it might help to chant a blessing or something?'

'Not unless Jarmoskowski overheard it – probably not even then, since we have no priest among us.'

'Very well. Pour, Bennington, before the goo hardens.'

Bennington decanted sluggishly molten silver into each depression in the clay, and Newcliffe cleaned away the oozy residue from the casts before it had time to thicken. At any other time the whole scene would have been funny – now it was grotesque, as if it had been composed by a Holbein. Newcliffe picked up the box and carried it back down to the cellar, where the emasculated cartridges awaited their new slugs.

'Who's going to carry these things, now?' Foote asked. 'There are six rifles. James, how about you?'

'I couldn't hit an elephant's rump at three paces. Tom's an expert shot. So is Bennington here, with a shotgun anyhow; he holds skeet-shooting medals.'

'I can use a rifle,' Bennington said diffidently.

'So can I,' said Palmer curtly. 'Not that I've got much sympathy for this business. This is just the kind of thing you'd expect to happen in this place.'

'You had better shelve your politics for a while,' James said, turning an unexpectedly hard face to the Labour MP. 'Lycanthropy as a disease isn't going to limit its activities to the House of Lords. Suppose a werewolf got loose in the Welsh coalfields?'

'I've done some shooting,' Foote said. 'During the show at Dunkirk I even hit something.'

'I,' Lundgren said, 'am an honorary member of the Swiss Militia.'

Nobody laughed. Even Palmer was aware that Lundgren in his own oblique way was bragging, and that he had something to brag about. Newcliffe appeared abruptly from the cellar.

'I pried 'em loose, cooled 'em with snow and rolled 'em smooth with a file. They're probably badly crystallized, but we needn't let that worry us. At worst it'll just make 'em go dum-dum on us – no one here prepared to argue that that would be inhumane, I hope?'

He put one cartridge into the chamber of each rifle in turn and shot the bolts home. 'There's no sense in loading these any more thoroughly – ordinary bullets are no good anyhow, Chris says. Just make your first shots count. Who's elected?'

Foote, Palmer, Lundgren and Bennington each took a rifle. Newcliffe took the fifth and handed the last one to his wife.

'I say, wait a minute,' James objected. 'Do you think that's wise, Tom? I mean, taking Caroline along?'

'Why, certainly,' Newcliffe said, looking surprised. 'She shoots like a fiend – she's snatched prizes away from me a couple of times. I thought *everybody* was going along.'

'That isn't right,' Foote said. 'Especially not Doris, since the wolf – that is, I don't think she ought to go.'

'Are you going to subtract a marksman from the hunting party to protect her? Or are you going to leave her here by herself?'

'Oh no!' Doris cried. 'Not here! I've got to go! I don't want to wait all alone in this house. He might come back, and there'd be nobody here. I couldn't stand it.'

'There is no telling what Jarmoskowski might learn from such an encounter,' Lundgren added, 'or, worse, what he might teach Doris without her being aware of it. For the rest of us – forgive me, Doris, I must be brutal – it would go harder with us if he did not kill her than if he did. Let us keep our small store of magic with us, not leave it here for Jan.'

'That would seem to settle the matter,' Newcliffe said grimly. 'Let's get under way. It's after two now.'

He put on his heavy coat and went out with the heavy-eyed groom to rouse out the dogs. The rest of the company fetched their own heavy clothes. Doris and Caroline climbed into ski-suits. They assembled again, one by one, in the living-room.

Lundgren's eyes swung on a vase of iris-like flowers on top of the closed piano. 'Hello, what are these?' he said.

'Monkshood,' Caroline informed him. 'We grow it in the greenhouse. It's pretty, isn't it? Though the gardener says it's poisonous.'

'Chris,' Foote said. 'That isn't – wolfbane, is it?'

The psychiatrist shook his head. 'I'm no botanist. I can't tell one aconite from another. But it doesn't matter; hyperpineals are allergic to the whole group. The pollen, you see. As in hay fever, your hyperpineal case breathes the pollen, anaphylaxis sets in, and—'

'The last twist of the knife,' James murmured.

A clamouring of dogs outside announced that Newcliffe was ready. With sombre faces the party filed out on to the terrace. For some reason all of them avoided stepping on the wolf's prints in the snow. Their mien was that of condemned prisoners on the way to the tumbrels. Lundgren took one of the sprigs of flowers from the vase.

The moon had long ago passed its zenith and was almost half-way down the sky, projecting the Bastille-like shadow of the house a long way out on to the grounds; but there was still plenty of light, and the house itself was glowing from cellar to tower room. Lundgren located Brucey in the milling, yapping pack and abruptly thrust the sprig of flowers under his muzzle. The animal sniffed once, then crouched back and snarled softly.

'Wolfbane,' Lundgren said. 'Dogs don't dislike the other aconites – basis of the legend, no doubt. Better fire your gardener, Caroline. In the end he may be the one to blame for all this happening in the dead of winter. Lycanthropy normally is an autumn affliction.'

James said:

'Even a man who says his prayers
Before he sleeps each night
May turn to a wolf when the wolfbane blooms
And the moon is high and bright.'

'Stop it, you give me the horrors,' Foote snapped angrily.

'Well, the dog knows now,' said Newcliffe. 'Good. It would have been hard for them to pick up the trail from hard snow, but Brucey can lead them. Let's go.'

The tracks of the wolf were clear and sharp in the ridged drifts. The snow had formed a hard crust from which fine, powdery showers of tiny ice-crystals were whipped by a fitful wind. The tracks led around the side of the house, as Bennington had reported, and out across the golf-course. The little group plodded grimly along beside them. The spoor was cold for the dogs, but every so often they would pick up a faint trace and go bounding ahead, yanking their master after them. For the most part, however, the party had to depend upon its eyes.

A heavy mass of clouds had gathered in the west over the Firth of Lorne. The moon dipped lower. Foote's shadow, knobby and attenuated, marched on before him and the crusted snow crunched and crackled beneath his feet. The night seemed unnaturally still and watchful, and the party moved in tense silence except for an occasional growl or subdued bark from the dogs.

Once the marks of the werewolf doubled back a short distance, then doubled again, as if the monster had turned for a moment to look back at the house before resuming his prowling. For the most part, however, the trail led directly towards the dark boundary of the woods.

As the brush began to rise around them they stopped by mutual consent and peered warily ahead, rifles lifted half-way, muzzles weaving nervously as the dogs' heads shifted this way and that. Far out across the countryside behind them, the great cloud-shadow continued its sailing. The brilliantly-lit house stood out against the gloom as if it were on fire.

'Should have turned those out,' Newcliffe muttered, looking back at it. 'Outlines us.'

The dogs strained at their leashes. In the black west there was a barely audible muttering, as of winter thunder. Brucey pointed a quivering nose at the woods and snarled.

'He's in there, all right.'

'We'd better step on it,' Bennington said, whispering. 'Going to be plenty dark in about five minutes. Looks like a storm.'

Still they hesitated, looking at the noncommittal darkness of the forest. Then Newcliffe waved his gun hand and his dog hand in the conventional deploy-as-skirmishers signal and ploughed forward. The rest spread out in a loosely spaced line and followed him. Foote's finger trembled over his trigger.

The forest was shrouded and very still. Occasionally a branch groaned as someone pushed against it, or twigs snapped with sharp, tiny, musical explosions. Foote could see almost nothing. The underbrush tangled his legs; his feet broke jarringly through the crust of snow, or were supported by it when he least expected support. Each time his shoulder struck an unseen trunk gouts of snow fell on him.

After a while the twisted, leafless trees began to remind him of something; after a brief mental search he found it. It was a Doré engraving of the woods of Hell, from an illustrated Dante which had frightened him green as a child: the woods where each tree was a sinner in which harpies nested, and where the branches bled when they were broken off. The concept still frightened him a little – it made the forest by Newcliffe's golf-course seem almost cosy.

The dogs strained and panted, weaving, no longer growling, silent with a vicious intentness. A hand touched Foote's arm and he jumped; but it was only Doris.

'They've picked up something, all right,' Bennington's whisper said. 'Turn 'em loose, Tom?'

Newcliffe pulled the animals to a taut halt and bent over them, snapping the leashes free. One by one, without a sound, they shot ahead and vanished.

Over the forest the oncoming storm-clouds cruised across the moon. Total blackness engulfed them. The beam of a powerful flashlight splashed from Newcliffe's free hand, flooding a path of tracks on the brush-littered snow. The rest of the night drew in closer about the blue-white glare. 'Hate to do this,' Newcliffe said. 'It gives us away. But he knows we're— Hello, it's snowing.'

'Let's go then,' Foote said. 'The tracks will be blotted out shortly.'

A many-voiced, clamorous baying, like tenor bugles, rang suddenly through the woods. It was a wild and beautiful sound. Foote, who had never heard it before, thought for an instant that his heart had stopped. Certainly he would never have associated so pure a choiring with anything as prosaic as dogs.

'That's it!' Newcliffe shouted. 'Listen to them! That's the view halloo. Go get him, Brucey!'

They crashed ahead. The belling cry seemed to ring all around them.

'What a racket!' Bennington panted. 'They'll raise the whole countryside.'

They ploughed blindly through the snow-filled woods. Then, without any interval, they broke through into a small clearing. Snowflakes flocculated the air. Something dashed between Foote's legs, snapping savagely, and he tripped and fell into a drift.

A voice shouted something indistinguishable. Foote's mouth was full of snow. He jerked his head up – and looked straight into the red rage-glowing eyes of the wolf.

It was standing on the other side of the clearing, facing him, the dogs leaping about it, snapping furiously at its legs. It made no sound at all, but stood with its forefeet planted, its head lowered below its enormous shoulders, its lips drawn back in a travesty of Jarmoskowski's smile. A white streamer of breath trailed horizontally from its long muzzle, like the tail of a malign comet.

It was more powerful than all of them, and it knew it. For an instant it hardly moved, except to stir lazily the heavy brush of tail across its haunches. Then one of the dogs came too close.

The heavy head lashed sideways. The dog yelped and danced back. The dogs already had learned caution: one of them already lay writhing on the ground, a black pool spreading from it, staining the snow.

'Shoot, in God's name!' James screamed.

Newcliffe clapped his rifle to his shoulder with one hand, then lowered it indecisively. 'I can't,' he said. 'The dogs are in the way—'

'To hell with the dogs – this is no foxhunt! Shoot, Tom, you're the only one of us that's clear—'

It was Palmer who shot first. He had no reason to be chary of Newcliffe's expensive dogs. Almost at the same time the dogs gave Foote a small hole to shoot through and he took it.

The double flat crack of the two rifles echoed through the woods and snow puffed up in a little explosion behind the wolf's left hind pad. The other shot – whose had come closest could never be known – struck a frozen tree-trunk and went squealing away. The wolf settled deliberately into a crouch.

A concerted groan had gone up from the party; above it Newcliffe's voice thundered, ordering his dogs back. Bennington aimed with inexorable care.

The werewolf did not wait. With a screaming snarl it launched itself through the ring of dogs and charged.

Foote jumped in front of Doris, throwing one arm across his own throat. The world dissolved into rolling pandemonium, filled with shouts, screams, snarls, and the frantic hatred of dogs. The snow flew thick. Newcliffe's flashlight fell and tumbled away, coming to rest at last on the snow on its base, regarding the tree-tops with an idiot stare.

Then there was the sound of a heavy body moving swiftly away. The noise died gradually.

'Anybody hurt?' James's voice asked. There was a general chorus of 'no's'.

'That's not good enough,' Bennington puffed. 'How does a dead man answer No? Let's have a nose-count.'

Newcliffe retrieved his flashlight and played it about, but the snowstorm had reached blizzard proportions, and the light showed nothing but shadows and cold confetti. 'Caroline?' he said anxiously.

'Yes, dear. Soaked, but here.'

'Doris? Good. Paul, where are you – oh, I see you, I think.

Ehrenberg? And Palmer? So; there you have it, Bennington. We didn't invite anybody else to this party – except—'

'He got away,' Bennington said ironically. 'Didn't like the entertainment. And the snow will cover his tracks this time. Better call your dogs back. Tom.'

'They're back,' Newcliffe said. He sounded a little tired, for the first time since the beginning of the trouble. 'When I call them off, they come off.'

He walked heavily forward to the body of the injured animal, which was still twitching feebly, as if trying to answer his summons. He squatted down on his hams and bent his shoulders, stroking the restlessly rolling head.

'So – so,' he said softly. 'So, Brucey. Easy – easy. So, Brucey – so.'

Still murmuring, he brought his rifle into position with one arm. The dog's tail beat once against the snow.

The rifle leapt noisily against Newcliffe's shoulder.

Newcliffe arose slowly, and looked away.

'It looks like we lose round one,' he said tonelessly.

V

It seemed to become daylight very quickly. The butler went phlegmatically around the house, snapping off the lights. If he knew what was going on he gave no sign of it.

Newcliffe was on the phone to London. 'Cappy? Tom here – listen and get this straight, it's damned important. Get Consolidated Warfare – no, no, not the Zurich office, they've offices in the City – and place an order for a case of ·30 calibre rifle cartridges – listen to me, dammit, I'm not through yet – with *silver slugs*. Yes, that's right – silver – and it had better be the pure stuff, too. No, not sterling, that's too hard for my purposes. Tell them I want them flown up, and that they've got to arrive here tomorrow . . . I don't care if it is impossible. Make it worth their while; I'll cover it. And I want it direct to the house here. On Loch Rannoch 20 kilometres due west of Blair Atholl . . . Of course you know the house but how will CWS's pilot unless you tell them? Now read it back to me.'

'Garlic,' Lundgren was saying to Caroline. She wrote it dutifully on her marketing list. 'How many windows does this house have? All right, buy one clove for each, and get a half-dozen tins of ground rosemary, also.'

He turned to Foote. 'We must cover every possibility,' he said sombrely. 'As soon as Tom gets off the line I will try to raise the local priest and get him out here with a drayload of silver crucifixes. Understand, Paul, there is a strong physiological basis beneath all that medieval mumbo-jumbo.

'The herbs, for example, are anti-spasmodics – they act rather as ephedrine does, in hay fever, to reduce the violence of the seizure. It's possible that Jan may not be able to maintain the wolf shape if he gets a heavy enough sniff.

'As for the religious trappings, their effects are perhaps solely psychological – and perhaps not, I have no opinion in the matter. It's possible that they won't bother Jan if he happens to be a sceptic in such matters, but I suspect that he's—' Lundgren's usually excellent English abruptly gave out on him. The word he wanted obviously was not in his vocabulary. '*Abergläubisch*,' he said. '*Craindre*.'

'Superstitious?' Foote suggested, smiling grimly.

'Is that it? Yes. Yes, certainly. Who has better reason, may I ask?'

'But how does he maintain the wolf shape at all, Chris?'

'Oh, that's the easiest part. You know how water takes the shape of the vessel it sits in? Well, protoplasm is a liquid. This pineal hormone lowers the surface tension of the cells; and at the same time it short-circuits the sympathetic nervous system directly through to the cerebral cortex, by increasing the efficiency of the cerebrospinal fluid as an electrolyte beyond the limits in which it's supposed to function—'

'Whoa there, I'm lost already.'

'I'll go over it with you later, I have several books in my luggage which have bearing on the problem which I think you should see. In any event, the result is a plastic, malleable body, within limits. A wolf is the easiest form because the skeletons are so similar. Not much pinearin can do to bone, you see. An ape would be easier still, but lycanthropes don't assume shapes outside their own ecology. A were-ape would be logical in Africa, but not here. Also, of course, apes don't eat people; there is the really horrible part of this disease.'

'And vampires?'

'Vampires,' Lundgren said pontifically, 'are people we put in padded cells. It's impossible to change the bony structure *that* much. They just think they are bats. But yes, that too is advanced hyperpinealism.

'In the last stages it is quite something to see. As the pinearin blood-level increases, the cellular surface tension is lowered so much that the cells literally begin to boil away. At the end there is just a – a mess. The process is arrested when the vascular systems no longer can circulate the hormone, but of course the victim dies long before that stage is reached.'

Foote swallowed. 'And there's no cure?'

'None yet. Palliatives only. Someday, perhaps, there will be a cure – but until then— Believe me, we will be doing Jan a favour.'

'Also,' Newcliffe was saying, 'drive over and pick me up six automatic rifles. No, not Brownings, they're too hard to handle. Get American T-47s. All right, they're secret – what else are we paying CWS a retainer for? What? Well, you might call it a siege. All right, Cappy. No, I won't be in this week. Pay everybody off and send them home until further notice. No, that doesn't include you. All right. Yes, that sounds all right.'

'It's a good thing,' Foote said, 'that Newcliffe has money.'

'It's a good thing,' Lundgren said, 'that he has me – and you. We'll see how twentieth-century methods can cope with this Middle Ages madness.'

Newcliffe hung up, and Lundgren took immediate possession of the phone.

'As soon as my man gets back from the village,' Newcliffe said, 'I'm going to set out traps. Jan may be able to detect hidden metal – I've known dogs that could do it by smell in wet weather – but it's worth a try.'

'What's to prevent his just going away?' Doris asked hopefully. The shadows of exhaustion and fear around her eyes touched Foote obscurely; she looked totally unlike the blank-faced, eager youngster who had bounded into the party in ski-clothes so long ago.

'I'm afraid you are,' he said gently. 'As I understand it, he believes he's bound by the pentagram.' At the telephone, where Lundgren evidently was listening to a different speaker with each ear, there was an energetic nod. 'In the old books, the figure is supposed to be a sure trap for demons and such, if you can lure or conjure them into it. And once the werewolf has seen his appointed partner marked with it, he feels compelled to remain until he has made the alliance good.

'Doesn't it – make you afraid of me?' Doris said, her voice trembling.

He touched her hand. 'Don't be foolish. There's no need for us to swallow all of a myth just because we've found that part of it is so. The pentagram we have to accept; but I for one reserve judgment on the witchcraft.'

Lundgren said 'Excuse me' and put one hand over the mouthpiece. 'Only lasts seven days,' he said.

'The compulsion? Then we'll have to get him before then.'

'Well, maybe we'll sleep tonight anyhow,' Doris said dubiously.

'We're not going to do much sleeping until we get him,' Newcliffe announced. 'I could boil him in molten lead just for killing Brucey.'

'Brucey!' Palmer snorted. 'Don't you think of anything but your damned prize dogs, even when all our lives are forfeit?' Newcliffe turned on him, but Bennington grasped his arm.

'That's enough,' the American said evenly. 'Both of you. We certainly don't dare quarrel among ourselves with this thing hanging over us. I know your nerves are shot. We're all in the same state. But dissension among us would make things just that much easier for Jan.'

'Bravo,' Lundgren said. He hung up the phone and rejoined them. 'I didn't have much difficulty in selling the good Father the idea,' he said. 'He was stunned, but not at all incredulous. Unfortunately, he has only crucifixes enough for our ground-floor windows, at least in silver; gold, he says, is much more popular. By the way, he wants a picture of Jan, in case he should turn up in the village.'

'There are no existing photographs of Jarmoskowski,' Newcliffe said positively. 'He never allowed any to be taken. It was a headache to his concert manager.'

'That's understandable,' Lundgren said. 'With his cell radiogens under constant stimulation, any picture of him would turn out over-exposed anyhow – probably a total blank. And that in turn would expose Jan.'

'Well, that's too bad, but it's not irreparable,' Foote said. He was glad to be of some use again. He opened Caroline's secretary and took out a sheet of stationery and a pencil. In ten minutes he had produced a head of Jarmoskowski in three-quarter profile, as he had seen him at the piano that last night so many centuries ago. Lundgren studied it.

'To the life,' he said. 'Tom can send this over by messenger. You draw well, Paul.'

Bennington laughed. 'You're not telling him anything he doesn't know,' he said. Nevertheless, Foote thought, there was considerably less animosity in the critic's manner.

'What now?' James asked.

'We wait,' Newcliffe said. 'Palmer's gun was ruined by that one hand-made slug, and Foote's isn't in much better shape. The one thing we can't afford is to have our weapons taken out of action. If I know Consolidated, they'll have the machine-made bullets here tomorrow, and then we'll have some hope of getting him. Right now we'll just have to lie doggo and hope that our defences are effective – he's shown that he's more than a match for us in open country.'

The rest looked at each other uneasily. Some little understanding of what it would be like to wait through helpless, inactive days and dog-haunted nights already showed on their faces. But before the concurrence of both master hunters – Newcliffe and Lundgren – they were forced to yield.

The conference broke up in silence.

When Foote came into the small study with one of the books Lundgren had given him, he was surprised and somewhat disappointed to find that both Caroline and Doris had preceded him. Doris was sitting on a hassock near the grate, with the fire warming her face, and a great sheaf of red-gold hair pouring down her back. Caroline, seated just behind her, was brushing it out with even strokes.

'I'm sorry,' he said. 'I didn't know you were in here. I had a little reading to do and this looked like the best place for it—'

'Why, of course, Paul,' Caroline said. 'Don't let us distract you in the least. We came in here for the fire.'

'Well, if you're sure it's all right—'

'Of course it's all right,' Doris said. 'If our talking won't annoy you—'

'No, no.' He found the desk with the gooseneck lamp on it, turned on the lamp, and put down the heavy book in the pool of light. Caroline's arm resumed its monotonous, rhythmic movement over Doris's bent head. Both of them made a wonderful study: Caroline no longer the long-faced hounds-and-horses Englishwoman in jodhpurs, but now the exactly opposite type, tall, clear-skinned, capable of carrying a bare-shouldered evening gown with enchanting naturalness, yet in both avatars clearly the wife of the same man; Doris transformed from the bouncing youngster to the preternaturally still virgin waiting beside the lake, her youth not so much emphasized as epiphanized by the maternal shape stroking her head.

But for once in his life he had something to do that he considered more pressing than making a sketch for an abstraction. He turned his back on them and sat down, paging through the book to the chapter Lundgren had mentioned. He would have preferred studying it with Lundgren at his side, but the psychiatrist, wiry though he was, felt his years as the hour grew late, and was now presumably asleep.

The book was hard going. It was essentially a summary of out-of-the-way psychoses associated with peasant populations, and it had been written by some American who assumed an intolerably patronizing attitude towards the beliefs he was discussing, and who was further handicapped by a lack of basic familiarity with the English language. Foote suspected that sooner or later someone like Lundgren was going to have to do the whole job over again from scratch.

Behind him the murmuring of the two women's voices blended with the sighing of the fire in the grate. It was a warm, musical sound, so soothing that Foote found himself nodding at the end of virtually every one of the book's badly constructed paragraphs, and forced to reread nearly every other sentence.

'I do believe you've conquered Tom completely,' Caroline was saying. The brush went crackle ... crackle ... through the girl's hair. 'He hates women who talk. About anything. That's hard on him, for he loves artists of all sorts, and so many of them are women, aren't they?'

... Within a few years I was able to show to a startled world that between sympathetic magic and the sympatheticomimetic rituals of childhood there are a distinct relationship, directly connectable to the benighted fantasies of Balkan superstition of which I have just given so graphic a series of instances. Shortly thereafter, with the aid of Drs Egk and Bergenweiser, I was able to demonstrate ...

'So many of them are pianists, anyhow,' Doris said. 'Sometimes I wish I'd taken to the harp, or maybe the bassoon.'

'Well, now, I sometimes feel that way about being a woman. There really is a great deal of competition abroad in the world. Your hair is lovely. That white part is so fashionable now that it's a pleasure to see one that's natural.'

'Thank you, Caroline. You've been very brave and kind. I feel better already.'

'I've never known a woman,' Caroline said, 'who didn't feel better with the tangles out of her hair. Does this affair really disturb you greatly?'

... in order to make it clear that this total misconception of the real world can have no REAL consequences

except in the mind of the ignorant. To explain the accounts of the deceived observers we must first of all assume . . .

'Shouldn't it? I wouldn't have taken it seriously for a moment a few days ago, but – well, we did go out to hunt for Jan, and there really doesn't seem to be much doubt about it. It is frightening.'

'Of course it is,' Caroline said. 'Still I wouldn't dream of losing my sleep over it. I remember when Brucey had the colic when he was five weeks old; London was being bombed at the same time by those flying things. Tom carried on terribly, and the house was full of refugees, which simply made everything more difficult. And Jan is really very sweet and he's been most effective in the World Federation movement, really one of the best speakers we've ever had; I can't imagine that he would hurt anyone. I know what Tom would do if he discovered he could turn himself into a wolf. He'd turn himself in to the authorities; he's really very serious-minded, and fills every week-end with these artists until one wonders if anybody else in the world is sane. But Jan has a sense of humour. He'll be back tomorrow laughing at us.'

Foote turned a page in the book, but he had given up everything but the pretence of reading it.

'Chris takes it very seriously,' Doris said.

'Of course, he's a specialist. There now, that should feel better. And there's Paul, studying his eyes out; I'd forgotten you were there. What have you found?'

'Nothing much,' Foote said, turning to look at them. 'I really need Chris to understand what I'm reading. I haven't the training to extract meaning out of this kind of study. I'll tackle it with him tomorrow.'

Caroline sighed. 'Men are so single-minded. Isn't it wonderful how essential Chris turned out to be? I'd never have dreamed that he'd be the hero of the party.'

Doris got up. 'If you're through with me, Caroline, I'm very tired. Good night, and thank you. Good night, Paul.'

'Good night,' Foote said.

'Quite through,' Caroline said. 'Good night, dear.'

Then it was deep night again. The snowstorm had passed, leaving fresh drifts, and the moon was gradually being uncovered. The clouds blew across the house towards the North Sea on a heavy wind which hummed under the gutters, rattled windows, ground together the limbs of trees.

The sounds stirred the atmosphere of the house, which was hot and stuffy because of the closed windows and reeking with garlic. It was not difficult to hear in them other noises less welcome. In the empty room next to Foote's there was the imagined coming and going of thin ghosts to go with them, and the crouched expectancy of a turned-down bed which awaited a curiously deformed guest – a guest who might depress its sheets regardless of the tiny glint of the crucifix upon the pillow.

The boundary between the real and the unreal had been let down in Foote's mind, and between the comings and goings of the cloud-shadows and the dark errands of the ghosts there was no longer any way of making a selection. He had entered the cobwebby borderland between the human and the animal, where nothing is ever more than half true, and only as much as half true for the one moment.

After a while he felt afloat on the stagnant air, ready to drift all the way across the threshold at the slightest motion. Above him, other sleepers turned restlessly, or groaned and started up with a creak of springs. Something was seeping through the darkness among them. The wind followed it, keeping a tally of the doors that it passed.

One.

Two.

Three. Closer now.

Four. The fourth sleeper struggled a little; Foote could hear a muffled squeaking of floorboards above his head.

Five.

Six. Who was six? Who's next? When?

Seven—

Oh my God, I'm next . . . I'm next . . .

He curled into a ball, trembling. The wind died away and there was silence, tremendous and unquiet. After a long while he uncurled, swearing at himself; but not aloud, for he was afraid to hear his own voice. Cut that out, now, Foote, you bloody fool. You're like a kid hiding from the trolls. You're perfectly safe. Lundgren says so.

Mamma says so.

How the hell does Lundgren know?

He's an expert. He wrote a paper. Go ahead, be a kid. Remember your childhood faith in the printed word? All right, then. Go to sleep, will you?

There goes that damned counting again.

But after a while his worn-down nerves would be excited no longer. He slept a little, but fitfully, falling in his dreams through such deep pits that he awoke fighting the covers and gasping for the vitiated, garlic-heavy air. There was a foulness in his mouth and his heart pounded. He threw off the blankets and sat up, lighting a cigarette with shaking hands and trying not to see the shadows the match-flame threw.

He was no longer waiting for the night to end. He had forgotten that there had ever been such a thing as daylight. He was waiting only to hear the low, inevitable snuffling that would tell him he had a visitor.

But when he looked out the window, he saw dawn brightening over the forest. After staring incredulously at it for a long while, he stubbed out his cigarette in the socket of the candlestick – which he had been carrying about the house as if it had grown to him – and fell straight back. With a sigh he was instantly in profound and dreamless sleep.

When he finally came to consciousness he was being shaken, and Bennington's voice was in his ears. 'Get up, man,' the critic was saying. 'No, you needn't reach for the candlestick – everything's OK thus far.'

Foote grinned and reached for his trousers. 'It's a pleasure to see a friendly expression on your face, Bennington,' he said.

Bennington looked a little abashed. 'I misjudged you,' he admitted. 'I guess it takes a crisis to bring out what's really in a man so that blunt brains like mine can see it. You don't mind if I continue to dislike your latest abstractions, I trust?'

'That's your function: to be a gadfly,' Foote said cheerfully. 'Now, what's happened?'

'Newcliffe got up early and made the rounds of the traps. We got a good-sized rabbit out of one of them and made Hassenpfeffer – very good – you'll see. The other one was empty, but there was blood on it and on the snow around it. Lundgren's still asleep, but we've saved scrapings for him; still there doesn't seem to be much doubt about it – there's a bit of flesh with coarse black hair on it—'

James poked his head around the doorjamb, then came in. 'Hope it cripples him,' he said, dexterously snaffling a cigarette from Foote's shirt pocket. 'Pardon me. All the servants have deserted us but the butler, and nobody will bring cigarettes up from the village.'

'My, my,' Foote said. 'You're a chipper pair of chaps. Nice sunrise, wasn't it?'

'Wasn't it, though.'

In the kitchen they were joined by Ehrenberg, his

normally ruddy complexion pale and shrunken from sleeplessness.

'Greetings, Hermann. How you look! And how would you like your egg?'

'*Himmel, Asch und Zwirn,* how can you sound so cheerful? You must be part ghoul.'

'You must be part angel – nobody human could be so deadly serious so long, even at the foot of the scaffold.'

'Bennington, if you burn my breakfast I'll turn you out of doors without a shilling. Hello, Doris; can you cook?'

'I'll make some coffee for you.' Newcliffe entered as she spoke, a pipe between his teeth. 'How about you, Tom?'

'Very nice, I'm sure,' Newcliffe said. 'Look – what do you make of this?' He produced a wad of architect's oiled tracing-cloth from his jacket pocket and carefully unwrapped it. In it were a few bloody fragments. Doris choked and backed away.

'I got these off the trap this morning – you saw me do it, Bennington – and they had hair on 'em then. Now look at 'em.'

Foote poked at the scraps with the point of his pencil. 'Human,' he said.

'That's what I thought.'

'Well, isn't that to be expected? It was light when you opened the trap, evidently, but the sun hadn't come up. The werewolf assumes human form in full daylight – these probably changed just a few moments after you wrapped them up. As for the hair – this piece here looks to me like a blood-stained sample of Jarmoskowski's shirt-cuff.'

'We've nipped him, all right,' Bennington agreed.

'By the way,' Newcliffe added, 'we've just had our first desertion. Palmer left this morning.'

'No loss,' James said. 'But I know how he feels. When this

affair is over, I'm going to take a month off at Brighton and let the world go to hell.'

'What? In the winter?'

'I don't care. I'll watch the tides come in and out in the w.c.'

'Just be sure to live to get there,' Ehrenberg said gloomily.

'Hermann, you are a black cloud and a thunderclap of doom.'

There was a sound outside. It sounded like the world's biggest tea-kettle. Something flitted through the sky, wheeled and came back. Foote went to the nearest window.

'Look at that,' he said, shading his eyes. 'An Avro jet – and he's trying to land here. He must be out of his mind.'

The plane circled silently, engines cut. It lost flying speed and glided in over the golf-course, struck, and rolled at breakneck speed directly for the forest. At the last minute the pilot groundlooped the ship expertly and the snow fountained under its wheels.

'By heaven, I'll bet that's Newcliffe's bullets!'

They pounded through the foyer and out on to the terrace. Newcliffe, without bothering to don coat or hat, ploughed away towards the plane. A few minutes later, he and the pilot came puffing into the front room, carrying a small wooden case between them. Then they went back and got another, larger but obviously not so heavy.

Newcliffe pried the first crate open. Then he sighed. 'Look at 'em,' he said. 'Shiny brass cartridges, and dull silver heads, machined for perfect accuracy – there's a study in beauty for you artist chaps. Where'd you leave from?'

'Croydon,' said the pilot. 'If you don't mind, Mr Newcliffe, the company said I was to collect from you. That's six hundred pounds for the weapons, two-fifty for the ammo and a hundred and fifty for me, just a thousand in all.'

'Fair enough. Hold on, I'll write you a cheque.'

Foote whistled. It was obvious – not that there had ever been any doubt about it – that Tom Newcliffe did not paint for a living.

The pilot took the cheque, and shortly thereafter the tea-kettle began to whistle again. From the larger crate Newcliffe was handing out brand-new rifles, queer ungainly things with muzzle brakes and disproportionately large stocks.

'Now let him come,' he said grimly. 'Don't worry about wasting shots. There's a full case of clips. As soon as you see him, blaze away like mad. Use it like a hose if you have to. This is a high-velocity weapon: if you hit him square anywhere – even if it's only his hand – you'll kill him from shock. If you get him in the body, there won't be enough of that area left for him to reform, no matter what his powers.'

'Somebody go wake Chris,' Bennington said. 'He should have lessons too. Doris, go knock on his door like a good girl.'

Doris nodded and went upstairs. 'Now this stud here,' Newcliffe said, 'is the fire-control button. You put it in this position and the gun will fire one shot and reload itself, like the Garand. Put it here and you have to reload it yourself, like a bolt-action rifle. Put it here and it goes into automatic operation, firing every shell in the clip, one after the other and in a hurry.'

'Thunder!' James said admiringly. 'We could stand off an army.'

'Wait a minute – there seem to be two missing.'

'Those are all you unpacked,' Foote pointed out.

'Yes, but there were two older models of my own. I never used 'em because it didn't seem sporting to hunt with such cannon. But I got 'em out last night on account of this trouble.'

'Oh,' Bennington said with an air of sudden enlightenment. 'I thought that thing I had looked odd. I slept with one last night. I think Lundgren has the other.'

'Where is Lundgren? Doris should have had him up by now. Go see, Bennington, and fetch back that rifle while you're at it.'

'Isn't there a lot of recoil?' Foote asked.

'Not a great deal; that's what the muzzle brake is for. But it would be best to be careful when you have the stud on fully automatic. Hold the machine at your hip, rather than at your shoulder – what's *that*!'

'Bennington's voice,' Foote said, his jaw muscles suddenly almost unmanageable. 'Something must be wrong with Doris.' The group stampeded for the stairs.

They found Doris at Bennington's feet in front of Lundgren's open door. She was perfectly safe; she had only fainted. The critic was in the process of being very sick. On Lundgren's bed something was lying.

The throat had been ripped out, and the face and all the soft parts of the body were gone. The right leg had been gnawed in one place all the way to the bone, which gleamed white and polished in the reassuring sunlight.

VI

Foote stood in the living-room by the piano in the full glare of all the electric lights. He hefted the T-47 and surveyed the remainder of the party, which was standing in a puzzled group before him.

'No,' he said, 'I don't like that. I don't want you all bunched together. String out in a line, please, against the far wall, so that I can see everybody.'

He grinned briefly. 'Got the drop on you, didn't I? Not a rifle in sight. Of course, there's the big candlestick behind you, Tom – aha, I saw you sneak your hopeful look at it – but I know from experience that it's too heavy to throw. I can shoot quicker than you can club me, too.' His voice grew ugly. '*And I will*, if you make it necessary. So I would advise everybody – including the women – not to make any sudden movements.'

'What's this all about, Paul?' Bennington demanded angrily. 'As if things weren't bad enough—'

'You'll see directly. Get into line with the rest, Bennington. *Quick!*' He moved the gun suggestively. 'And remember what I said about moving too suddenly. It may be dark outside, but I didn't turn on all the lights for nothing.'

Quietly the line formed. The eyes that looked at Foote were narrowed with suspicion of madness, or something worse.

'Good. Now we can talk comfortably. You see, after what happened to Chris I'm not taking any chances. That was partly his fault, and partly mine. But the gods allow no one to err twice in matters of this kind. He paid for his second error – a price I don't intend to pay, or to see anyone else here pay.'

'Would you honour us with an explanation of this error?' Newcliffe said icily.

'Yes. I don't blame you for being angry, Tom, since I'm your guest. But you see I'm forced to treat you all alike for the moment. I was fond of Lundgren.'

There was silence for a moment, then a thin indrawing of breath from Bennington. 'All alike?' he whispered raggedly. 'My God, Paul. Tell us what you mean.'

'You know already, I see, Bennington. I mean that Lundgren was not killed by Jarmoskowski. He was killed by someone else. Another werewolf – yes, we have two now. One of them is standing in this room at this moment.'

A concerted gasp went up.

'Surprised?' Foote said, coldly, and deliberately. 'But it's true. The error for which Chris paid so dearly, an error which I made too, was this: we forgot to examine everyone for injuries after the encounter with Jan. We forgot one of the cardinal laws of lycanthropy.

'A man who survives being bitten by a werewolf himself becomes a werewolf. That's how the disease is passed on. The pinearin in the wolf's saliva evidently gets into the blood-stream, stimulates the victim's own pineal gland, and—'

'But nobody was bitten, Paul,' Doris said in a suspiciously reasonable voice.

'Somebody was, even if only lightly. None of you but Chris and myself could have known about the bite-infection. Evidently somebody got a few small scratches, didn't think them worth mentioning, put iodine on them and forgot about them – until it was too late.'

There were slow movements in the line – heads turning surreptitiously, eyes swinging to neighbours left and right.

'Paul, this is merely a hypothesis,' Ehrenberg said. 'There is no reason to suppose that it is so, just because it sounds likely.'

'But there is. Jarmoskowski can't get in here.'

'Unproven,' Ehrenberg said.

'I'll prove it. Once the seizure occurred, Chris was the logical first victim. The expert, hence the most dangerous enemy. I wish I had thought of this before lunch. In any event, if I'm right, Chris's safeguards against letting Jarmoskowski in also keep you from getting out. If you think you'll ever leave this room again, you're bloody wrong—'

He gritted his teeth and brought himself back into control. 'All right,' he said. 'This is the end of the line. Everybody hold up both hands in plain view.'

Almost instantly there was a ravening wolf in the room.

Only Foote, who could see at one glance the order of the people in the staggered line, could know who it was. His drummed-up courage, based solely on terror, went flooding out of him on a tide of sick pity; he dropped the rifle and began to weep convulsively. The beast lunged for his throat like a reddish projectile.

Newcliffe's hand darted back and grasped the candlestick. He leapt forward with swift clumsy grace and brought it down, whistling, against the werewolf's side. Ribs burst with a sharp splintering sound. The wolf spun, its haunches hitting the floor. Newcliffe hit it again. It fell, screaming like a great dog run down by a car, its fangs slashing the air.

Three times, with scientific viciousness, Newcliffe heaved the candlestick back and struck at its head. Then it cried out in an almost-familiar voice, and died.

Slowly the cells of its body groped back towards their natural positions. Even its fur moved, becoming more matted, more regular – more fabric-like.

The crawling metamorphosis was never completed; but the hairy-haunched thing with the crushed skull which sprawled at Newcliffe's feet was recognizable.

It had been Caroline Newcliffe.

Tears coursed along Foote's palms, dropped from under them, fell to the carpet. After a while he dropped his hands. Blurrily he saw a frozen tableau of wax figures in the yellow lamplight. Bennington's face was grey with illness, but rigidly expressionless, like a granite statue. James's back was against the wall; he watched the anomalous corpse as if waiting for some new movement. Ehrenberg had turned away, his pudgy fists clenched.

As for Newcliffe, he had no expression at all. He merely stood where he was, the bloody candlestick hanging straight down from a limp hand.

His eyes were quite empty.

After a moment Doris walked over to Newcliffe and touched his shoulder compassionately. The contact seemed to let something out of him. He shrank visibly into himself, shoulders slumping, his whole body withering to a dry husk.

The candlestick thumped against the floor, rocked wildly on its base, toppled across the body. As it struck, Foote's cigarette butt, which had somehow remained in its socket all day, tumbled out and rolled crazily along the carpet.

'Tom,' Doris said softly. 'Come away now. There's nothing you can do.'

'It was the blood,' his empty voice said. 'She had a cut. On her hand. Handled the scrapings from the trap. My trap. I did it to her. Just a breadknife cut from making canapes. I did it.'

'No you didn't, Tom. You're not to blame. Let's get some rest.'

She took his hand. He followed her obediently, stumbling a little as his spattered shoes scuffed over the thick carpet, his breath expelling from his lungs with a soft whisper. The french doors closed behind them.

Bennington bolted for the kitchen sink.

Foote sat down on the piano bench, his worn face taut with dried tears. Like any non-musician he was drawn almost by reflex to pick at the dusty keys. Ehrenberg remained standing where he was, so motionless as to absent himself from the room altogether, but the lightly struck notes aroused James. He crossed the room, skirting the body widely, and looked down at Foote.

'You did well,' the novelist said shakily. 'Don't condemn yourself, Paul. What you did was just and proper – and merciful in the long run.'

Foote nodded. He felt – nothing. Nothing at all.

'The body?' James said.

'Yes. I suppose so.' He got up from the bench. Together

they lifted the ugly shape; it was awkward to handle. Ehrenberg remained dumb, blind and deaf. They manoeuvred their way through the house and on out to the greenhouse.

'We should leave her here,' Foote said, the inside of his mouth suddenly sharp and sour. 'Here's where the wolfbane bloomed that started the whole business.'

'Poetic justice of sorts, I suppose,' James said. 'But I don't think it's wise. Tom has a toolshed at the other end that isn't steam heated. It should be cold enough there.'

Gently they lowered the body to the cement floor, laid down gunnysacks and rolled it on to them. There seemed to be nothing available to cover it. 'In the morning,' Foote said, 'we can have someone come for her.'

'How about legal trouble?' James said, frowning. 'Here's a woman whose skull has been crushed with a blunt instrument—'

'I think we can get Lundgren's priest to help us there, and with Lundgren too,' Foote said sombrely. 'Besides, Alec – is that a woman? Inarguably it isn't Caroline.'

James looked sideways at the felted, muscular haunches. 'No. It's – legally it's nothing. I see your point.'

Together they went back into the house. 'Jarmoskowski?' James said.

'Not tonight, I imagine. We're all too tired and sick. And we do seem to be safe enough in here. Chris saw to that.'

Ehrenberg had gone. James looked around the big empty room.

'Another night. What a damnable business. Well, good night, Paul.'

He went out. Foote remained in the empty room a few minutes longer, looking thoughtfully at the splotch of blood on the priceless Persian carpet. Then he felt his face and throat, looked at his hands, arms and legs, and explored his chest under his shirt.

Not a scratch. Tom had been very fast.

He was exhausted, but he could not bring himself to go to bed. With Lundgren dead, the problem was his; he knew exactly how little he knew about it still, but he knew as well how much less the rest of the party knew. Hegemony of the house was his now – and the next death would be his responsibility.

He went around the room, making sure that all the windows were tightly closed and the crucifixes in place, turning out the lights as he went. The garlic seemed to be effective. He clicked out all but the last light, picked up his rifle and went out into the hall.

Doris's room door was open and there was no light coming out of it. Evidently she was still upstairs tending Newcliffe. He stood for a few moments battling with indecision, then toiled up the staircase.

He found her in Caroline's room, her head bowed upon her arm among the scattered, expensive vials and flasks which had been Caroline's armamentarium. The room was surprisingly *frou-frou*; even the telephone had a doll over it. This, evidently, had been the one room in the house which Caroline had felt was completely hers, where her outdoorsy, estate-managing daytime personality had been ousted by her nocturnal femininity.

And what, in turn, had ousted that? Had the womanly Caroline been crowded, trying not to weep, into some remote and impotent corner of her brain as the monster grew in her? What did go on in the mind of a werewolf?

Last night, for instance, when she had brushed Doris's hair, she had seemed completely and only herself, the Caroline Newcliffe with the beautiful face and the empty noggin towards whom Foote had so long felt a deep affection mixed with no respect whatsoever. But she had already been taken. It made his throat ache to realize that in her matronly hovering over the girl there had already been some of the tenseness of the stalker.

Men are so single-minded. Isn't it wonderful how essential Chris turned out to be?

At that moment she had shifted her target from Doris to Chris, moved by nothing more than Foote's remark about being unable to progress very far without the psychiatrist. Earlier this evening he had said that Chris had been the most logical target because he was the expert – yet that had not really occurred to Caroline except as an afterthought. It was wolf-reasoning; Caroline's own mind had seen danger first in single-mindedness.

And it had been Caroline's mind, not the wolf's, which had dictated the original fix on Doris. The girl, after all, was the only other woman in the party, thanks to Tom's lion-hunting and his dislike of the Modern Girl; and Caroline had mentioned that Tom seemed drawn to Doris. Which was wolf, which human? Or had they become blended, like two innocuous substances combining to form a poison? Caroline had once been incapable of jealousy – but when the evil had begun to seethe in her blood-stream she had been no longer entirely Caroline . . .

He sighed. Doris had seemed to be asleep on the vanity, but she stirred at the small sound, and the first step he took across the threshold brought her bolt upright. Her eyes were reddened and strange.

'I'm sorry,' he said. 'I was looking for you. I have to talk to you, Doris; I've been putting it off for quite a while, but I can't do that any longer. May I?'

'Yes, of course, Paul,' she said wearily. 'I've been very rude to you. It's a little late for an apology, but I am sorry.'

He smiled. 'Perhaps I had it coming. How is Tom?'

'He's – not well. He doesn't know where he is or what he's doing. He ate a little and went to sleep, but he breathes very strangely.' She began to knead her hands in her lap. 'What did you want?'

'Doris – what about this witchcraft business? Lundgren seemed to think it might help us. God knows we need help. Have you any idea why Chris thought it was important? Beyond what he told us, that is?'

She shook her head. 'Paul, it seemed a little silly to me then, and I still don't understand it. I can do a few small tricks, that's all, like the one I did to you with the smoke. I never thought much about them; they came more or less naturally, and I thought of them just as a sort of sleight-of-hand. I've seen stage conjurers do much more mystifying things.'

'But by trickery – not by going right around natural law.'

'What do I know about natural law?' she said reasonably. 'It seems natural to me that if you want to make something plastic behave, you mould something else that's plastic near by. To make smoke move, you move clay, or something else that's like smoke. Isn't that natural?'

'Not very,' he said wryly. 'It's a law of magic, if that's any comfort to either of us. But it's supposed to be a false law.'

'I've made it work,' she said, shrugging.

He leaned forward. 'I know that. That's why I'm here. If you can do that, there should be other things that you can do, things that can help us. What I want to do is to review with you what Chris thought of your talents, and see whether or not anything occurs to you that we can use.'

She put her hands to her cheeks, and then put them back in her lap again. 'I'll try,' she said.

'Good for you. Chris said he thought witches in the old days were persons with extra-sensory perception and allied gifts. I think he believed also that the magic rituals that were used in witchcraft were just manipulative in intention – symbolic objects needed by the witch to focus her extra-sensory powers. If he was right, the "laws" of magic really were illusions, and what was in operation was something much deeper.'

'I think I follow that,' Doris said. 'Where does it lead?'

'I don't know. But I can at least try you on a catalogue. Have you ever had a prophetic dream, Doris? Or read palms? Or cast horoscopes? Or even had the notion that you could look into the future?'

She shook her head decidedly.

'All right, we'll rule that out. Ever felt that you knew what someone else was thinking?'

'Well, by guesswork—'

'No, no,' Foote said. 'Have you ever felt certain that you knew—'

'Never.'

'How about sensing the positions of objects in another room or in another city – no. Well, have you ever been in the vicinity of an unexplained fire? A fire that just seemed to happen because you were there?'

'No, Paul, I've never seen a single fire outside of a fireplace.'

'Ever moved anything larger and harder to handle than a column of smoke?'

Doris frowned. 'Many times,' she said. 'But just little things. There was a soprano with a rusty voice that I had to accompany once. She was overbearing and a terrible stage hog. I tied her shoe-bows together so that she fell when she took her first bow, but it was awfully hard work; I was all in a sweat.'

Foote suppressed an involuntary groan. 'How did you do it?'

'I'm not quite sure. I don't think I could have done it at all if we hadn't wound up the concert with *Das Buch der Hängenden Gärten.*' She smiled wanly. 'If you don't know

Schoenberg's crazy counterpoint that wouldn't mean anything to you.'

'It tells me what I need to know, I'm afraid. There really isn't much left for me to do but ask you whether or not you've ever transformed a woman into a white mouse, or ridden through the air on a broomstick. Doris, doesn't *anything* occur to you? Chris never talked without having something to talk about; when he said that you could help us, he meant it. But he's dead now and we can't ask him for the particulars. It's up to you.'

She burst into tears. Foote got clumsily to his feet, but after that he had no idea what to do.

'Doris—'

'I don't know,' she wailed. 'I'm not a witch! I don't want to be a witch! I don't know anything, anything at all, and I'm so tired and so frightened and please go away, please—'

He turned helplessly to go, then started to turn back again. At the same instant, the sound of her weeping was extinguished in the roar of an automatic rifle, somewhere over their heads, exhausting its magazine in a passionate rush.

Foote shot out of the room and back down the stairs. The ground floor still seemed to be deserted under the one light. Aloft there was another end-stopped snarl of gunfire; then Bennington came bouncing down the stairs.

'Watch out tonight,' he panted as soon as he saw Foote. 'He's around. I saw him come out of the woods in wolf form. I emptied the clip, but he's a hard target against those trees. I sprayed another ten rounds around where I saw him go back in, but I'm sure I didn't hit him. The rifle just isn't my weapon.'

'Where were you shooting from?'

'The top of the tower.' His face was very stern. 'Went up for a breath and a last look around, and there he was. I hope he comes back tonight. I want to be the one who kills him.'

'You're not alone.'

'Thank God for that. Well, good night. Keep your eyes peeled.'

Foote stood in the dark for a while after Bennington had left. Bennington had given him something to think about. While he waited, Doris picked her way down the stairs and passed him without seeing him. She was carrying a small, bulky object; since he had already put the light out, he could not see what it was. But she went directly to her room.

I want to be the one who kills him.

Even the mild Bennington could say that now; but Foote, who understood the feeling behind it all too well, was startled to find that he could not share it.

How could one hate these afflicted people? Why was it so hard for equal-minded men like Bennington to remember that lycanthropy was a disease like any other, and that it struck its victims only in accordance with its own etiology, without regard for their merits as persons? Bennington had the reputation of being what the Americans called a liberal, all the way to his bones; presumably he could not find it in his heart to hate an alcoholic or an addict. He knew also – he had been the first to point it out – that Jarmoskowski as a human being had been compassionate and kindly, as well as brilliant; and that Caroline, like the poor devil in Andreyev's *The Red Laugh*, had been noble-hearted and gentle and had wished no one evil. Yet he was full of hatred now.

He was afraid, of course, just as Foote was. Foote wondered if it had occurred to him that God might be on the side of the werewolves.

The blasphemy of an exhausted mind; but he had been unable to put the idea from him. Suppose Jarmoskowski should conquer his compulsion and lie out of sight until the seven days were over. Then he could disappear; Scotland was large and sparsely populated. It would not be necessary for him to kill all his victims thereafter – only those he actually needed for food. A nip here, a scratch there—

And then from wherever he hunted, the circle of lycanthropy would grow and widen and engulf—

Perhaps God had decided that proper humans had made a muddle of running the world; had decided to give the *nosferatu*, the undead, a chance at it. Perhaps the human race was on the threshold of that darkness into which he had looked throughout last night.

He ground his teeth and made a noise of exasperation. Shock and exhaustion would drive him as crazy as Newcliffe if he kept this up. He put his hands to his forehead, wiped them on his thighs, and went into the little study.

The grate was cold, and he had no materials for firing it up again. All the same, the room was warmer than his bed would be at this hour. He sat down at the small desk and began to go through Lundgren's book again.

Cases of stigmata. Accounts of Sabbats straight out of Krafft-Ebing. The dancing madness. Theory of familiars. Conjuration and exorcism. The besom as hermaphroditic symbol. Fraser's Laws. Goetha as an international community. Observations of Lucien Levy-Bruehl. The case of Bertrand. Political commentary in *Dracula.* Necromancy v. necrophilia. Nordau on magic and modern man. Basic rituals of the Anti-Church. Fetishism and the theory of talismans . . .

Round and round and round, and the mixture as before. Without Chris there was simply no hope of integrating all this material. Nothing would avail them now but the rifles with the silver bullets in them; their reservoir of knowledge of the thing they fought had been destroyed.

Foote looked tiredly at the ship's clock on the mantel over the cold grate. The fruitless expedition through the book had taken him nearly two hours. He would no longer be able to avoid going to bed. He rose stiffly, took up the automatic rifle, put out the light, and went out into the cold hall.

As he passed Doris's room, he saw that the door was now just barely ajar. Inside, two voices murmured.

Foote was an incurable eavesdropper. He stopped and listened.

VII

It was years later before Foote found out exactly what had happened at the beginning. Doris, physically exhausted by her hideous day, emotionally drained by tending the child-like Newcliffe, feeding him from a blunt spoon, parrying his chant about traps and breadknives, and herding him into bed, had fallen asleep almost immediately. It was a sleep dreamless except for a vague, dull undercurrent of despair. When the light tapping against the window-panes finally reached through to her, she had no idea how long she had been lying there.

She struggled to a sitting position and forced her eyelids up. Across the room the moonlight, gleaming in patches against the rotting snow outside, glared through the window. Silhouetted against it was a tall human figure. She could not see its face, but there was no mistaking the red glint of its eyes. She clutched for her rifle and brought it awkwardly into line.

Jarmoskowski did not dodge. He moved his forearms out a little way from his body, palms forward in a gesture that looked almost supplicating, and waited. Indecisively she lowered the gun again. What was he asking for?

As she dropped the muzzle she saw that the fire-control stud was at *automatic*. She shifted it carefully to *repeat*. She was afraid of the recoil Newcliffe had mentioned; she could feel surer of her target if she could throw one shot at a time at it.

Jarmoskowski tapped again and motioned with his finger. Reasoning that he would come in of his own accord if he were able, she took time out to get into her housecoat. Then, holding her finger against the trigger, she went to the window. All its sections were closed tightly, and a crucifix, suspended from a silk thread, hung exactly in the centre of it. She touched it, then opened one of the small panes directly above Jarmoskowski's head.

'Hello, Doris,' he said softly. 'You look a little like a clerk behind that window. May I make a small deposit, miss?'

'Hello.' She was more uncertain than afraid. Was this really happening, or was it just the recurrent nightmare? 'What do you want? I should shoot you. Can you tell me why I shouldn't?'

'Yes, I can. Otherwise I wouldn't have risked exposing myself. That's a nasty-looking weapon.'

'There are ten silver bullets in it.'

'I know that too. I had some fired at me earlier tonight. And I would be a good target for you, so I have no hope of escape – my nostrils are full of rosemary.' He smiled ruefully. 'And Lundgren and Caroline are dead, and I am responsible. I deserve to die; that is why I am here.'

'You'll get your wish, Jan,' she said. 'But you have some other reason, I know. I'll back my wits against yours. I want to ask you questions.'

'Ask.'

'You have your evening clothes on. Paul said they changed with you. How is that possible?'

'But a wolf has clothes,' Jarmoskowski said. 'He is not naked like a man. And surely Chris must have spoken of the effect of the pineal upon the cell radiogens. These little bodies act upon any organic matter, wool, cotton, linen, it hardly matters. When I change, my clothes change with me. I can hardly say how, for it is in the blood – the chromosomes – like musicianship, Doris. Either you can or you can't. If you can – they change.'

'Jan – are there many like you? Chris seemed to think—'

Jarmoskowski's smile became a little mocking. 'Go into a great railroad station some day – Waterloo, or a Metro station, or Grand Central in New York; get up above the crowd on a balcony or stairway and look down at it in a mirror. We do not show in a silvered mirror. Or if you are in America, find one of the street photographers they have there who take "three action pictures of yourself" against your will and try to sell them to you; ask him what percentage of his shots show nothing but background.'

His voice darkened gradually to a sombre *diapason*. 'Lundgren was right throughout. This werewolfery is now nothing but a disease. It is not pro-survival. Long ago there must have been a number of mutations which brought the pineal gland into use; but none of them survived but the werewolves, and the werewolves are madmen – like me. We are dying out.

'Some day there will be another mutation, the pineal will come into better use, and all men will be able to modify their forms without this terrible cannibalism as a penalty. But for us, the lycanthropes, the failures of evolution, nothing is left.

'It is not good for a man to wander from country to country, knowing that he is a monster to his fellow-men and cursed eternally by his God – if he can claim a God. I went through Europe, playing the piano and giving pleasure, writing music for others to play, meeting people, making friends – and always, sooner or later, there were whisperings and strange looks and dawning horror.

'And whether I was hunted down for the beast I was, or

whether there was only a gradually growing revulsion, they drove me out. Hatred, silver bullets, crucifixes – they are all the same in the end.

'Sometimes, I could spend several months without incident in some one place, and my life would take on a veneer of normality. I could attend to my music, and have people around me that I liked, and be – human. Then the wolfbane bloomed and the pollen freighted the air, and when the moon shone down on that flower my blood surged with the thing I carry within me—

'And then I made apologies to my friends and went north to Sweden, where Lundgren was and where spring came much later. I loved him, and I think he missed the truth about me until the night before last; I was careful.

'Once or twice I did *not* go north, and then the people who had been my friends would be hammering silver behind my back and waiting for me in dark corners. After years of this, few places in Europe would have me. With my reputation as a composer and a pianist spread darker rumours, none of them near the truth, but near enough.

'Towns I had never visited closed their gates to me without a word. Concert halls were booked up too many months in advance for me to use them, inns and hotels were filled indefinitely, people were too busy to talk to me, to listen to my playing, to write me any letters.

'I have been in love. That – I will not describe.

'Eventually I went to America. There no one believes in the werewolf. I sought scientific help – which I had never sought from Lundgren, because I was afraid I would do him some harm. But overseas I thought someone would know enough to deal with what I had become. I would say, "I was bitten during a hunt on Graf Hrutkai's estate, and the next fall I had my first seizure—"

'But it was not so. No matter where I go, the primitive

hatred of my kind lies at the heart of the human as it lies at the heart of the dog. There was no help for me.

'I am here to ask for an end to it.'

Slow tears rolled over Doris's cheeks. The voice faded away indefinitely. It did not seem to end at all, but rather to retreat into some limbo where men could not hear it. Jarmoskowski stood silently in the moonlight, his eyes burning bloodily, a sombre sullen scarlet.

Doris said, 'Jan – Jan, I am sorry, I am so sorry. What can I do?'

'Shoot.'

'I – can't!'

'Please, Doris.'

The girl was crying uncontrollably. 'Jan, don't. I can't. You know I can't. Go away, *please* go away.'

Jarmoskowski said, 'Then come with me, Doris. Open the window and come with me.'

'Where?'

'Does it matter? You have denied me the death I ask. Would you deny me this last desperate hope for love, would you deny your own love, your own last and deepest desire? That would be a vile cruelty. It is too late now, too late for you to pretend revulsion. Come with me.'

He held out his hands.

'Say good-bye,' he said. 'Good-bye to these self-righteous humans. I will give you of my blood and we will range the world, wild and uncontrollable, the last of our race. They will remember us, I promise you.'

'Jan—'

'I am here. Come now.'

Like a somnambulist, she swung the panes out. Jarmoskowski did not move, but looked first at her, then at the crucifix. She lifted one end of the thread and let the little thing tinkle to the floor.

'After us, there shall be no darkness comparable to our darkness,' Jarmoskowski said. 'Let them rest – let the world rest.'

He sprang into the room with so sudden, so feral a motion that he seemed hardly to have moved at all. From the doorway an automatic rifle yammered with demoniac ferocity. The impact of the silver slugs hurled Jarmoskowski back against the side of the window. Foote lowered the smoking muzzle and took one step into the room.

'Too late, Jan,' he said stonily.

Doris wailed like a little girl awakened from a dream. Jarmoskowski's lips moved, but there was not enough left of his lungs. The effort to speak brought a bloody froth to his mouth. He stood for an instant, stretched out a hand towards the girl. Then the long fingers clenched convulsively and the long body folded.

He smiled, put aside that last of all his purposes, and died.

'Why did he come in?' Foote whispered. 'I could never have got a clear shot at him if he'd stayed outside.'

He swung on the sobbing girl. 'Doris, you must tell me, if you know. With his hearing, he should have heard me breathing. But he stayed – and he came in, right into my line of fire. *Why?*'

The girl did not answer; but stiffly, as if she had all at once become old, she went to her bedside light and turned it on. Standing beneath it was a grotesque figurine which Foote had difficulty in recognizing as Caroline's telephone doll. All the frills had been stripped off it, and a heavy black line had been pencilled across its innocuous forehead in imitation of Jarmoskowski's eyebrows. Fastened to one of its wrists with a rubber band was one of the fragments of skin Newcliffe had scraped out of his trap; and completely around the doll, on the surface of the table, a pentagram had been drawn in lipstick.

The nascent witch had turned from white magic to black. Doris had rediscovered the malign art of poppetry, and had destroyed her demon lover.

Compassionately, Foote turned to her; and very slowly, as if responding to the gravitational tug of a still-distant planet, the muzzle of his rifle swung too. Together, the man and the machine, they waited for her.

Both would have to be patient.